Mira Falling

Maria Arena

ISBN 978-0-9925479-3-6

MIRA (mi-r-ah): 'The Wonder Star' or The Amazing One'

Excerpt from Grade Ten SOS paper written by Mira Falling:

Mira (Omicron Ceti) can be found in the constellation Cetus and is the brightest of the red class M 'long period variables' stars. It has a 330-day cycle during which it is sometimes visible to the human eye. With a temperature of 2000 degrees Kelvin, Mira is the coolest star in the galaxy. However, it is approaching the last stages of its life and will soon burn out and be lost to interstellar space.

Kaler, J. (No date) Mira

Available: www.astro.uiuc.edu/-kaler/sow/mira.htm

'I don't know why I done what I done. The way I done it, I seen it on TV shows. I had my own way, though. Simple and easy. No one would hear them scream.'

Christine Falling (19 years old)
Convicted of murdering three children (1982)

'I wanted to become known, to get myself a name.'

Robert Smith (18 years old)
Convicted of murdering five women and two children in a beauty salon (1966)

PRELUDE

One of the new girls asked me, just the other day, if I knew exactly where and when my career began. I thought about that question for a long time. Why had no one asked it before? It seemed to me to be a most important question, maybe the only one that mattered. Yet, in all the time that I've been here, during all of the sessions I've attended, it had never come up. Not even once.

I took my time considering Casey's question (or was it Tracy? I can never remember since most of the bimbos here are so totally forgettable). I thought back, turning events over in my mind. Finally, I told her I believed it had started on a hot summer's afternoon, on the headland above Beachmere, the little fishing village not far from my home town of Harvest Bay.

The headland (Disaster Point on the map) juts into the ocean like a crooked finger, gnawed ragged by the pounding waves. On its windswept knoll, there is a lighthouse and a keeper's cottage surrounded by long grass and pockets of scruffy trees. A short walk from the lighthouse is a safety fence, which crowns the headland like a tiara, and is meant to prevent the unlucky, the desperate and the stupid from falling over the sheer cliffs onto the rocks far below.

It is a stunningly beautiful place. If the day is clear, you can almost see New Zealand floating on the horizon. The ocean sparkles like blue crystal as it washes onto the beaches that stretch to the north and south while, behind the lighthouse, the Great Dividing Range lurks in deep green shadow.

It wasn't the headland's natural beauty that attracted us, though. We (Jack, Alyce, Danny and me) didn't give a damn about that. We went there because it was a place where we could hang out and be ourselves -where we could play war games in the long grass; or practise the drawback behind the lighthouse; or stand on the edge of the cliff and think about suicide when it seemed that our lives had turned to shit.

Our parents didn't like us going to the headland. They said it was too dangerous, but we knew they'd done their share of fooling around up there when they were kids. Everyone in town had. If you didn't spend at least one summer exploring the headland and dangling some part of your body over the cliffs, you weren't considered a local. It was like a rite of passage; one that our parents had conveniently forgotten about when they banned us from going there. As if that would stop us.

The thing is - though I wouldn't admit it back then - they were right. It was a dangerous place, for some people.

But not for me.

For me, the headland was a place where I could cut loose and have some fun; where I could play my little games (like the one I invented the summer of my twelfth birthday) and not stress about the consequences. It was a place where I could be a bit daring, maybe, a bit reckless; a place to do *anything* that would relieve the boredom that was a permanent part of living in a small town like Harvest Bay.

ONE

The idea for the game came to me while I was watching Jack and Danny toss rocks off the headland into the swirling ocean below. I stubbed out my cigarette on the lighthouse wall and looked over at Alyce, who was blowing smoke rings into the air, which the breeze torn apart the moment they left her puckered lips.

'Back in a sec,' I said, climbing to my feet. She lifted an eyebrow and released another perfect white-grey circle. I waved my hand through it, beating the wind to its disintegration, and then wandered down to the wooden safety fence where the boys were arguing over their rock-throwing prowess.

When Jack saw me, he grabbed my arm. 'You saw it, didn't you, Mira? My rock went all the way out there, near where that gull's flying,' he said, his hand wandering over the horizon. He folded his arms across his thin chest and grinned smugly.

'No way,' Danny challenged. 'Mine went heaps further than his, didn't it, Mira?'

'I don't know, maybe. Why don't you both throw again?' I suggested, picking a couple of rocks out of the pile they'd collected and slipping them into their hands. 'But wait until I'm ready, okay.' They nodded in unison, their hair ruffling in the wind whipping over the bluff.

There was a wildness to that wind that always made me feel sort of skittish and untameable. I took a deep breath, sucking salty air into my lungs and grinned at the cormorant that shot over the rocks as it surfed the slipstream. I loved it on the headland. It felt like the top of the world and was an eternity away from the dull universe of grown-ups, school and responsibility.

The others loved it too. It held such an attraction for us that at least three times a week during the summer break, when the days bulged with possibilities, we'd ride our bikes the eight kilometres from Harvest Bay to Beachmere, despite the blistering heat. Thankfully, it was an easy ride. The road was straight and the traffic was always light, except just before 'Happy Hour', when the fishermen from Beachmere headed into Harvest Bay for their nightly drinking session.

They weren't a problem for us 'cause we'd leave the Bay early in the morning when the heat of the day was still bearable. If we were lucky, there'd be a fresh breeze slipping through the scrub from the ocean. If we were unlucky, the wind would rise out of the west.

On these days, the stench from the rubbish dump that lay halfway between the Bay and Beachmere would sit across the road like a toxic fog. With no way to avoid the sickly-sweet smell, we'd ride as fast as we could, one hand clamped over our noses, until we'd burst (groaning with relief) into the fresh air on the other side.

Although we hated the dump, the wildlife - including a few people - loved it. Rats, snakes and feral cats snacked on the garbage, while fat midnight-black crows with sharp golden eyes, smoky grey seagulls and sneaky mynah birds squabbled noisily over last week's pizza crusts. Yet, as numerous as these creatures were, the true kings of the rubbish heap were the ibis.

Each morning, hundreds of dirty white, black-beaked birds would swoop in from their nesting trees in perfect bomber-squadron formation, calling raucously as they fluttered down among the debris. They'd spend the day roaming and scratching with their long, skinny legs as they searched for anything edible. Then in the afternoon, as if a knock-off whistle had sounded, they'd take flight again, back to their roosts, black spots against the pink-tinged sky.

Sometimes we'd ride our bikes down the shadowed alleyways between the mountains of rubbish, screaming like brawling cats, just to scare the ibis from their disgusting work. But mostly we were happy to leave the dump and its army of scavengers behind us.

Once we reached Beachmere, we'd chain our bikes up behind the surf club and go hiking along the beach. Jack and Danny always raced ahead; their lean shadows stretched out behind them, making them seem much taller than their ten years. They'd stop to look in the tidal pools, poking and prodding anything that dared to move, while Alyce and I collected shells and talked about school and boys.

The first jellyfish missile was always a warning. It'd land in front of us, splashing wet sand and small blobs of brown spongy flesh over our legs. Down the beach, our brothers prepared for war - a jellyfish in each hand, more collected at their feet. There was no point in running, unless we wanted to feel those cold slimy bodies slithering down our backs. So we'd grab the first jellyfish and throw it back, its thick tentacles spinning as it turned over and over. Suddenly, the air would be full of gelatinous shapes, sailing across the beach and dropping around us with sticky splats.

When we got too hot to throw, or avoid, the jelly-fish, we'd race into the ocean and go body surfing, washing away the mushy remains of our war.

By mid-afternoon, we'd be starving so we'd head back to the surf club and buy hot chips and Cokes. Then we'd walk up to the top of the headland where Alyce and I would smoke the cigarettes I'd nicked from Dad, while the boys amused themselves playing commando in the long grass or hunting for cicadas in the salt-stunted trees.

I didn't often get involved in what the boys were doing - I was too mature for their games - but some-times when a good idea occurred to me, I felt obliged to initiate them into the fun that life had to offer. The game I had in mind on that particular afternoon was one of my better ones, and as I squatted down and searched for a rock that would sit comfortably in my palm, they watched me with wide-eyed curiosity and expectation.

As I stood up, Alyce came down the slope from the lighthouse. 'What are you doing?' she asked.

'Grab a rock, Alyce. I've just thought up a new game.'

'What sort of game?' she asked, cautiously. She was the sensible one; the one who kept us out of trou-ble.

Well, mostly.

'A fun game,' I said, rolling my eyes. 'Come on, just choose a rock, will you?' She frowned but bent down and picked up a small rock only slightly bigger than a pebble. 'Could you have found a smaller one?' I asked.

She looked down at the pile. 'Probably,' she replied.

I shook my head and walked down to the safety fence, with the boys close behind me and Alyce dragging her feet at the rear. Before they could stop me, I quickly climbed over the barrier.

'What are you doing?' Jack wanted to know.

'Playing my game,' I said, taking a step away from the railing.

'For God's sake, you idiot, get back over here.' Alyce's dark eyes flashed impatiently and then widened as her brother scrambled over the fence too. 'Danny! No! Damn it, Mira, look what you've done now,' she shouted.

'So how do we play?' Danny asked, stepping onto the ledge beside me.

'I'll explain in a minute, but first we need two more players.' I took his hand as the wind roared up the rock face and buffeted our bodies. It swirled beneath my hair and under my arms, as if it wanted to lift me from the earth and send me flying over the ocean.

I smiled at my brother and Alyce encouragingly but, like always, they needed convincing. God, if it weren't for me, they'd never have any fun.

'Come on, Jackie. What's the matter? Scared?' I asked.

He glared at me, and then climbed over the railing. I hid a smile behind my hand. If there was one thing I could rely on, it was that Jack couldn't resist a challenge. It was what made him such a great runner.

'Come over here, Danny,' he said, as his feet touched the ground. Danny released my hand and walked over to Jack. They stood by the fence, but didn't try to climb back over and I knew Jack was hooked.

'Well, what about it, Alyce? Are you gonna climb over? Or are you too *good* to join in?' I taunted.

Alyce stuck her middle finger up and then scrambled over the fence.

I knew she'd take the bait. Alyce hated being called a goodie-goodie, even though she was one. She worked hard in school and spent hours practising her flute, getting every note perfect. When she wasn't studying or rehearsing, she was helping in her dad's pizza shop, usually as the waitress but sometimes making the pizzas. No matter what she did, though, the customers loved her because she was so (sickeningly) polite and considerate.

Then there was the way she looked out for Danny. Alyce was the perfect little mum. (Her mum, Mrs Parish, had died a couple of years before.) She always made sure no one hassled Danny for being 'special' - he was a bit slow when it came to learning stuff - and helped him to cope with life.

Although Alyce behaved like a saint, she wouldn't admit to being one and, just to prove that she wasn't too perfect, she'd sometimes do stuff that was a bit reckless - like climbing onto a ledge high above the ocean. I smiled to myself. She was so bloody predictable.

Now that Alyce was on the ledge, I explained the game. It was simple, really. We'd take turns throwing the rocks into the ocean and whoever threw the farthest would take a step towards the edge of the cliff. Whoever got closest to the edge, without taking a step back, would win.

'That's it? That's your game?' Jack asked, unconvinced. 'That's the stupidest thing you've ever come up with.'

'You don't have to play,' I replied, as a gust of wind lashed the headland.

Alyce brushed her long brown hair out of her face. 'Jack's right, Mira, that really is a dumb idea.'

'It is not,' I replied, turning away from them and taking a step towards the edge.

'Mira!' Jack yelled.

'Come on, Mira, let's climb back over,' Alyce said, her voice rising.

I ignored them and took another step. The cliff's jagged edge filled my vision and I felt my heart speed up, just a little. I could hear scuffling noises behind me, and then Danny yelled, 'Let go of me. I want to play Mira's game too.'

'No, Danny. It's stupid and dangerous,' Jack said, his voice wavering between anger and fear.

'But, Mira's playing.'

'That's because she's stupid. And dangerous.'

'That's not a very nice thing to say about your sister, Jack,' I said, looking over my shoulder. 'Remind me to thump you later. Okay?'

'Sure, but how are you gonna thump me when you're lying at the bottom of the cliff in a bloody heap?' Jack demanded.

I ignored him and took another tiny step.

Toes on the edge. The wind whistling in my ears, plucking at my clothes, urging me forward. Panicked voices behind me, demanding that I step back from the precipice.

In the end, it was my dream - and Jack - that saved me.

As I stood on the lip of the headland, mesmerised by the sight of the rocks and the rushing ocean below, my dreams of stardom crowded into my head. It just wouldn't be right for me to die now. Two minutes of fame on the evening news wouldn't make me a star. If I was going to die young, I wanted to be famous first. So famous the world would never forget me.

I looked down at the stone resting loosely in my hand and made my decision. I swung my arm behind me, ready to throw the rock into the sea. Suddenly, I felt my body shift as the small pebbles slid from beneath my feet and the world began to tilt. But, just as it seemed that my uneventful and - worse - unsuccessful life was about to end, Jack yanked me away from the edge. I flew backwards and landed on top of him, driving the air from his lungs. I rolled away and lay on my back, breathing rapidly; my heart pounding like a tom-tom, laughing wildly at the sky.

'Shut up,' Alyce yelled, as she helped Jack to his feet and guided him to the safety fence. His face was white and he coughed as he gulped at the salty air. When he looked at me, his blue eyes were as hard as chips of ice.

Leaning on Alyce, Jack dragged himself over the railing and walked slowly up the slope to the lighthouse with Danny trudging behind him. Alyce remained by the fence, staring furiously down at me.

'Guess I kind of spoiled the day, huh?' I said, trying to stifle the laughter that bubbled in my throat.

She didn't answer me straight away but looked out to sea, choosing her words. 'You're my best friend, Mira, but if you ever put Danny in danger or do a stupid thing like that again, I'll forget I ever knew you. Understand?'

'Oh, come on, Alyce. It was just a bit of fun.'

'No,' she said, firmly. 'It wasn't fun. It was suicidal.'

'Oh, don't be so frigging dramatic,' I replied, standing up and brushing dirt from my board shorts. 'You're just shitty 'cause you didn't think of it yourself.'

Alyce stared at me with eyes as cold as mud. 'I'm taking Danny and Jack home. Don't bother tagging along.'

'Fine, piss off then,' I shouted, as she walked towards the lighthouse. 'It was just a bloody game!'

If Alyce had a flaw it was that she was so damn stubborn when she was mad about something, and she was really mad after that day on the headland. Two whole weeks passed before she would answer my messages and phone calls or talk to me at school. She gave in eventually (after much begging) but she made me promise never to play my game again and, to save our friendship, I never did.

Well, not with Jack, Alyce and Danny, anyway.

ITEM ONE

Email #1

Retrieved from hard drive belonging to: Mira Falling (Age 18)

Point of Origin and Authorship Indeterminable

From: <nkelly@thegretamob.com>
To: <fallingstar@email.com.au>
Sent: Friday, 31 September 2008 8:45 PM.
Subject: Fw: Outlaw Legends

Dear Miss Falling,

I wish to acquaint you with the deceiver of your brother. Her cruelty demands a speedy dispatch to Kingdom Come. They will brand you the blackest and coldest-blooded murderer on record, as they called me, but we shall endure, you and I, in the legends of our land.

N.K.

Assessment: A search of the (3) computer terminals used by the Falling family failed to definitively pinpoint the genesis of the N.K. email. (Note: N.K. appears to refer to the notorious Australian outlaw, Ned Kelly.) However, it seems most likely that the origin was the computer terminal located in the bedroom of Jack Falling.

TWO

When Jack turned eleven, he sprouted wings and began to fly. We always knew he was a fast runner - he
could beat Dad (who wasn't all that fit anyway) over
a hundred metres when he was ten - but then suddenly, almost overnight, no one could catch him.

He left his mates for dead when they played
footy and could out run any of the high school guys
who wanted to belt him up for being a smart arse.
When Mum needed him to go to the shop for milk, he
wouldn't ride his bike like a normal kid; he'd run, just
for the thrill of moving fast.

It was after the school athletics carnival, when
Jack came home with a swag of blue ribbons, that
Dad started looking at him in a new way. Suddenly
his head was filled with dreams of Olympic gold and
glory, and he was determined that those dreams
would come true for Jack (which would take care of a
few of his own as well).

Dad started Jack on a training program and entered him in every running competition around the
district until a scout from the Australian Institute of
Sport spotted him at the Junior National Champion-
ships. The scout, Mr Anderson or something, was

impressed with Jack's athletic abilities and he told Dad that he was 'scholarship material', a comment that only encouraged my dad to push Jack harder than ever before:

'Lengthen that stride, boy.'

'Keep your eyes on the finish line, son.'

'Check the watch, mate. I know you can go faster.'

I felt sorry for Jack sometimes (at least until I realised that his running could get me out of the Bay). It was like watching that scene at the beginning of Gallipoli, where the uncle is training Archie:

'What are your legs?' his uncle demands.

'Springs. Steel springs.'

'What are they going to do?'

'Hurl me down the track.'

'How fast can you run?'

'As fast as a leopard.'

'How fast *are* you going to run?'

'As *fast* as a leopard.'

The difference between Archie and Jack, which Dad didn't know, or refused to see, was that Jack hated running competitively. He loathed the hours spent jogging through the streets of the Bay and sprinting along the beach in preparation for competition. He detested the weekend meets - the pressure of always having to prove himself - but mostly, he hated the never-ending dissection of his races, stride by boring stride, on the way home in the car.

I hated that too.

Jack still did it though, week after week, because it made Dad happy (all that dutiful son crap, I guess), but it didn't change the fact that running bored him to death.

I was in my room one afternoon, trying to figure out who'd sent me the weird email that had just turned up in my mailbox, when Jack stumbled through the door and collapsed on the floor. 'I don't want to do this anymore,' he moaned.

'So, don't,' I said, squinting at the computer screen. Who the hell *was* N.K.?

'I have to. Dad'll have a heart attack.'

'No, he won't. Just tell him that you're sick of all this running crap and that you really want be a writer instead.'

I read through the email again and checked the address. Who was it from? It was definitely for me, but what was it supposed to mean? Was it talking about Jack? Maybe it was from some religious nut - they were the only people who talked about Kingdom Come, weren't they?

'Yeah, right,' Jack said, rolling onto his back. 'Then Dad *really* would have a heart attack.'

'So?'

Jack shook his head. 'That's nasty, Mira.'

'No, it's not. You want to be a writer, so be a writer. What's he going to do? Beat you up? Kick you out of home? I don't think so.'

'It's not that easy, and you know it,' Jack said, dragging himself off the floor as Mum called out from the kitchen, telling us to wash up for dinner.

I sighed and closed my mail program. Jack was right. It wasn't easy for him. He was the one with the talent - my parents assumed that I didn't have any - and he was the one they'd pinned all their hopes on. It was a burden I happily let him carry. I spun around on my chair. 'Well, then, stop whining,' I said. 'Just do your best and we'll both get out of here. Sooner or later.'

He smiled as he shuffled out of my room and we both knew he'd be up at five, trying to outrun the stopwatch and our father's dreams.

The one thing Jack *did* like about running was his training buddy, Sally Millar. He had a crush on that girl the size of Uluru. A few months after they started training together, he bought Sally the cutest white rabbit for her birthday, which she - *sooo* creatively - named Snowdrop. It cost him a month's pocket money, but Jack didn't care, especially after Sally showed her appreciation with a kiss.

He wore a dopey smile on his face for a week after that. At least until he heard that Sally was going around with one of the boys from the caravan park, a tourist from Sydney.

God, was he ever cut up about that.

Jack could be bloody annoying sometimes but he was still my baby brother and he didn't deserve that sort of treatment. Besides, it was really depressing having someone moping around the house all day.

Then, about a week after the great break-up, Jack got a call from Sally. She was blubbering about her rabbit and how someone had crushed the poor little thing to death. She wanted Jack to go to the funeral that her family was holding for it in their backyard and, although he thought it was kind of pathetic, he agreed to go.

I wasn't invited but, since I had nothing better to do with my afternoon, I decided that I would secretly tag along.

There was something intriguing about the idea of a pet burial. I don't know if it was 'cause I'd recently finished reading *Pet Sematary* (a pass-on from Alyce, who just couldn't get enough of the 'Master' as she reverently called Stephen King. I always got the giggles when she spoke about him that way; as though he was the Dalai Lama of trashy horror novels). Or maybe it was that my dad refused to let us have any pets of our own.

It wasn't that he didn't like animals - he always donated cans of food to the local animal refuge - but every time Jack or I brought up the question of a pet, or worse, tried to smuggle some pitiful creature into the house, Dad would go off like a firecracker with a faulty fuse.

'Get rid of it!' he'd yell, flapping his newspaper at Jack, or me depending on who was holding the offending animal. 'You know this is an animal-free zone. I've got enough to do without feeding that bloody thing. And don't try to tell me that you'll look after it; we all know that won't happen and it'll be me or your mother who ends up caring for the wretched thing while you two nick off down the beach or something.'

We'd look at him with wide, imploring eyes. 'Forget it! If you want a pet, I'll buy you a framed photograph of one. At least then we won't have to feed it or clean up after it, and we'll be able to go on holidays whenever we want without worrying about what we're going to do with it.' He'd turn from us, still muttering as he shook his fist towards the front door, and stomped off to his favourite spot of the veranda, as though the mere presence of an animal in his house caused him great offence.

The closest Jack and I came to owning a pet was a blue tongue lizard that made its home among the rocks of the retaining wall that ran alongside our driveway about a year before Sally's rabbit took its last bite of the carrot. I saw the lizard from my bedroom window one morning as it slipped out of a dark crevice between two boulders, its indigo tongue flicking as it tasted the air for the scents of prey and danger. Fascinated, I watched as it crawled onto a smooth area of rock and lay there soaking up the sun, its shiny scales gleaming like fragments of polished onyx.

From my doorway, Jack let out a jaw-cracking yawn and I raised my hand, both calling him to me and demanding his silence, without looking away from the lizard. He stood behind me and leaned over my shoulder, following my finger as I pointed out of the window. I heard him draw in a sharp breath and I glanced at him, grinning.

We watched the lizard every day for a week. Jack insisted that we give it a name, though I thought the idea was pretty lame; it was a lizard after all. After much debate and rejected ideas, he came up with Inky.

'Are you serious?' I asked.

'What's wrong with that?'

'Nothing,' I said, covering the smirk on my face. 'It's lucky lizards have such small brains.'

'They're not the only ones with small brains,' Jack said, and hissed as I pinched the tender flesh at the back of his arm.

A few days later, Jack started feeding Inky steak that he pilfered from the kitchen, which was really the beginning of the end for our lizard friend. I tried to warn Jack but he wouldn't listen. He insisted that Inky wasn't getting enough to eat and so he'd cut the steak into small chunks that he would leave on the rock. Then he would sit, a little Buddha in our drive-way, and wait for Inky to come out of his hiding place, drawn by the smell of raw meat sweating in the afternoon sun.

The lizard would scoop up the scraps with his sticky bruise-coloured tongue, small black eyes re-garding Jack without fear before scurrying away, leaving the remaining meat to draw the ants and flies and, eventually, our dad's attention.

I came home from school one afternoon to find Dad poking around the wall with a stick. He saw me as I came into my room and called me over to my window. The scowl on his face told me all I needed to know.

'What's this dried meat doing here, Mira?'

I shrugged. 'I think Jack's been feeding some-thing.'

The scowl deepened and he jabbed the stick de-terminedly into the shadowed cracks. I turned away, hoping Inky had an escape route at the back of the retaining wall but, although I watched for him to make his usual afternoon appearance, his rock re-mained vacant and somehow desolate, like a stage without an actor.

That night at dinner, Dad fixed Jack and I with a stern glare; the one that always makes me quiver in-side like a small girl ready to burst into tears 'cause her daddy is angry with her. 'No pets means no pets, domestic, native or otherwise. Do I make myself clear?'

As we muttered our agreement, I glanced at Jack and saw the misery on his face. He knew Inky was gone and that he was responsible for his demise. My heart went out to him and when our dad got up from the table, I leant over and said, 'Don't take it so hard, Jackie. It was just a lizard.'

There was a glint in his eyes and his bottom lip trembled as he lowered his head and concentrated on his plate. I looked at him for a moment longer, then shrugged and stabbed my fork into a piece of broccoli. As I chewed, I thought about Inky and Jack.

I couldn't understand why he was so cut up about a lizard. Despite what our dad said, there would be other pets in his life, even if he had to wait until he was an adult to own one. Why did people get so attached to things? Didn't they know that everything in life was temporary? Except maybe for fame - the famous lived forever; just look at Elvis.

The same question occurred to me as I followed Jack over to Sally's place. What was so special about Snowdrop? It was a rabbit for God's sake, not the frigging Pope. Yet Sally was acting as though it was her best friend or favourite movie star who had died. And what did she hope to achieve by giving it a proper burial? Entry into rabbit heaven? Or, as the 'Master' would have it, resurrection with a downside? It made little sense to me; why not just toss out the body with the rest of the rubbish? I sighed and quickened my pace as Jack disappeared around the corner.

The Millar family lived three streets over from us on Acacia Drive. Next to their house was a vacant block, overgrown with wild grass and dotted with scraggly bushes. Beside the Millar's fence grew a small but leafy mulberry tree, heavy with fruit. I sat in the shadows beneath the tree, eating the juicy berries, while I watched the ceremony.

Jack and Sally stood together beside a pile of dirt, in a shady corner of her backyard. Next to the dirt was a shoebox, covered in white cloth, and a small cross made out of two crooked sticks held together with bright red electrical tape. On the other side of the grave stood Sally's parents, their heads bowed.

After a quiet moment, Sally pulled a piece of paper from the back pocket of her shorts and began to read. There was a lot of sentimental crap about Snowdrop being a good rabbit and his 'soft pink nose' and 'dewy eyes' — blah, blah, blah.

When she'd finished reading, Sally turned to Jack. 'Although Snowdrop wasn't with me for very long, I'm glad that I had him. Thank you, Jack,' she said and kissed him quickly on the cheek. Then she started to sob, as though the world was going to end, and stumbled around the box to where her mother stood. Mrs Millar guided her towards the house, leaving Jack with Mr Millar.

I could tell from the way he kind of shuffled his feet that the whole thing embarrassed Jack, but he helped Mr Millar clean up anyway. When they'd finished, Jack snapped a bottlebrush flower from a nearby tree and put it on the grave. Then he and Mr Millar went into the house.

Later that afternoon, I slipped into Jack's bedroom. He was lying on the floor, his head resting next to the vibrating speaker of his stereo system. When he saw me, he pushed a button on the remote and the music dipped to a low thumping hum.

'So, who do you think did in poor Peter Rabbit?' I asked, flipping through a surfing magazine.

'Snowdrop,' Jack said. He looked troubled and tired, and I wondered if he was hiding something from me.

'Okay, *Snowdrop*,' I conceded. 'How's Sally doing?'

'She'll be okay. And, no, I don't know who killed her rabbit.'

'Oh come on, the Millar's must have some idea.'

'What do you want to hear, Mira?' Jack snapped. 'That some psycho rabbit killer broke into their backyard and squeezed Snowdrop until his eyes popped from their sockets? Or that Sally found him rammed up the back of his cage like a bloody rag?'

'Hey, don't bite my head off. I was just asking if they knew who did it, that's all.'

'Well, they don't. And even if they did, it probably wouldn't matter because they've decided to move out of the Bay, anyway.'

'Really? Just 'cause of a rabbit?'

'No. They're putting Sally into a special athletics school in Brisbane. They were going to leave at the end of the year but after this, they've decided to go now.'

'Is that why you're hiding in your room? Are you all upset 'cause the girl of your dreams is moving away?' I fluttered my eyelids.

'Piss off,' Jack muttered, turning his music up.

We never found out who killed Snowdrop and the Millar's left the Bay for good a week later. But that wasn't the last time Sally played a part in our lives. And it wasn't the last time that Jack was involved with a death in the Bay. Not that he killed that poor little bunny. He's my little brother, after all, and I know exactly what he can and what he can't do.

ITEM TWO

Email #2

Retrieved from hard drive belonging to: Mira Falling (Age 18)

Point of Origin and Authorship Indeterminable

From: <saucyjack@fromhell.com>

To: <fallingstar@email.com.au>

Sent: Friday, 6 June 2009 7:16 PM

Subject: Fw: The Road to Fame

Dear Falling Star,

I know the secrets of your heart. Set them free and you, like me, will be a legend for all time. Play my funny little games, make the sweet blood flow. My knife was nice and sharp, good for ripping. Find your way and let the good times begin. You will be a star.

Yours truly,

Saucy Jack.

Assessment: The origins of the Saucy Jack email remain unclear. 'Saucy Jack' was allegedly the pseudonym used by a late 19th-century murderer, Jack the Ripper, however, no connection is made here between the activities of Mira Falling and the infamous Whitechapel criminal. The email was recovered from a hard drive that also contained the N.K. email (as well as several others). It is believed that the same author is responsible for both pieces of correspondence.

THREE

Every small town has someone like Mrs Johnson. She's the kind old lady who takes in stray animals and stray children, feeding them on gingernut cookies, milk and heaps of grandmotherly love. She's the wise old woman who people turn to for advice because she survived a war or two and the Harvest Bay heatwave of 1964. She's the 'dear heart' that everyone puts up with - even when she drives her ancient Morris Minor at twenty kilometres an hour down the centre of the road, causing a traffic jam in the middle of summer - because, as my dad would say, she's a *living treasure*.

More like a fossilised shark, I reckon. All dried up and brittle, but still with those wickedly sharp teeth made for snapping off heads.

Mrs Johnson lived across the street from us in a large mud-brown house that her husband had bought when Madonna was a baby. Mum told me once that it was the first house built in our part of the Bay, and it looked like it too, especially after Mr Johnson took a one-way trip to the Pearly Gates.

We were in the middle of dinner one night when Mum dropped the bombshell on us. She wanted Jack and me to go over to Mrs Johnson's on Saturday mornings to help with her chores. Mum continued to spew out the usual parent babble about it being a charitable thing to do and how it would teach us to be less selfish. Jack (the cretin) just shrugged and agreed, but I was against it from the start.

'You can't do this to me, Mum. I'm fourteen. I have a social life. I can't waste my Saturdays over there.'

Dad looked up from his steak and said, 'It's only for a couple of hours, sweetheart.'

'So you're both in on this? Great, what are you trying to do? Ruin my life?'

'Of course not. We just think it would be good for you to interact with an older person in our community.'

'But she hates me,' I wailed.

'Don't be so dramatic, Mira,' Mum said, with the serenity of someone who knows their decision is final. 'Mrs Johnson is too sweet to hate anyone. Besides, if you don't help her out, there'll be no social life for the rest of the weekend.'

'This is so unfair,' I yelled as I stormed off to my room, knowing I'd be across the street at eight, just like they wanted.

God, I hated Saturday mornings. Old Mrs Johnson was about as sweet as a green lemon. She'd follow me around the house, whining about how careless I was or nagging me for being too slow. Nothing I did was ever good enough, and some days I just wanted to strangle her with one of those ugly knee-high stockings she always wore.

Jack never seemed bothered about helping her out. He'd do whatever she wanted and, in return, she gave him the fun jobs, like trimming the trees or painting her front door, while I got stuck with the crap jobs like cleaning her bathroom. Gross!

He was her favourite (what's new?) and she re-warded him every week with batches of her double chocolate muffins. It used to make me sick watching Jack stuffing muffin after muffin into his mouth, fattening up on globs of gooey cake, while Mrs Johnson cackled and cooed over his greediness.

She wasn't laughing, though, the day she busted him - and the rest of us - drinking in her back shed.

We'd been hanging out at the break-wall with some of the older kids from town when Pete Middleton rocked up with a case of beer. Alyce glanced at me nervously and tipped her head towards home. She didn't like being around Pete and his mates when they started drinking. I couldn't blame her. They were cool guys when they were straight but once they got into a few beers, they were little more than pigs. I nodded and looked around for Jack and Danny.

They were standing near the beer, nudging each other in the ribs. I frowned, wondering what the hell they were up to. Suddenly, Jack dipped into the box and pulled out two bottles of beer. He passed one to Danny, who quickly hid it under his shirt, and slipped the other bottle into a deep pocket in his cargo shorts. Then, proving he had balls bigger than an elephant, he called out to Pete and waved as they casually strolled away.

I grabbed Alyce by the arm and dragged her after them. 'Hey,' I called, when we were far enough away from the older kids, 'what have you got in your pants, Jack Falling?'

He turned around and regarded me with wide

innocent eyes. 'Nothing,' he replied.

'It doesn't look like nothing to me.' I clicked my tongue and shook my head regretfully. 'You know, Pete's going to kill you when he figures out that his case is two bottles short. So, why don't you give the beer to us and we'll take it back? Maybe we can even talk him into going easy on you.'

Jack grinned. 'No way. You just want the beer for yourself.'

Alyce stamped her foot on the ground. I looked over at her and was surprised to see that her face was filled with anger. She went up to Danny, took the beer from under his shirt and slipped it into her backpack. 'You shouldn't take stuff that doesn't belong to you. It's stealing,' she told him.

Danny stared at his shoes. 'I know that,' he muttered.

Then she turned to Jack. 'And you shouldn't encourage him to do the wrong thing.' She held out her hand and Jack reluctantly gave her the other bottle, which she slipped inside her backpack. She gripped the bag tightly in her arms, as if she expected Jack to try and snatch it from her, and started walking up the road. I watched her for a second and then I jogged after her. When I got to her side, I was even more surprised to find her smiling. 'What the hell was that about?' I asked, confused.

Alyce shrugged and walked a little faster. 'He wasn't going to give it to you,' she said, and burst out laughing as we started to run.

'Damn it, she tricked us,' Jack yelled, giving chase. Danny let out a blood-curdling howl that would have impressed the savages in *The Lord of the Flies* and raced after him.

Alyce and I dodged into the laneway that ran behind Mrs Johnson's house, just as Jack and Danny caught up with us. We fell into the long grass, laughing and coughing at the same time, trying to get our breath back.

Jack pulled the backpack out of Alyce's hand. He took a beer out and held it up to the late afternoon sun. Large air bubbles foamed at the bottle's neck. 'Well, that's stuffed,' he said.

'You didn't really mean to drink it, did you?' Alyce asked, sitting up. She began to pick grass seeds from the back of her brother's shirt.

'Why else would we take it?' Jack said.

Danny absently lifted his arm so that Alyce could reach the seeds stuck along his side. His eyes followed the bottle in Jack's hand. 'We're still going to drink it, aren't we, Jack? You said, 'beer tastes good' - his voice changed as he mimicked Jack - 'and I want to try it.'

'We'll all try it, Danny,' I said, as I stood up and took the bottle from Jack. 'It's a bit frothy but I heard that makes the alcohol work faster.'

Jack screwed up his face. 'Who told you that?'

'I don't know. I just heard it somewhere. Anyway, we can't drink it out here where someone might see us. So, where should we go?'

Jack came up with the idea of Mrs Johnson's shed. It was a run-down building covered in creeping ivy that was tucked away in the corner of her yard, close to the back fence. Jack had been in there a few times, to get gardening tools and painting stuff, and he knew where she kept the key.

'But we'd better hurry up 'cause I don't want to be looking for the key in the dark,' he said, climbing the fence.

I followed Jack over and then Danny dropped down beside me. Last over was Alyce. 'What if Mrs Johnson finds us?' she whispered.

Jack was standing on a log of wood beside the door. He ran his fingers along the overhang until he found the key. He grinned at us and jumped down, cat-silent, among the weeds.

'Mrs Johnson never comes down here,' he reassured Alyce as he slid the key into the lock and pulled the door open. It let out a thin shriek and we froze, our eyes glued to the back of Mrs Johnson's house.

When nothing moved, we crept inside the shed, leaving the door open to avoid making any more noise. I cracked open the first beer and stifled a giggle as it foamed over my hand and onto the floor. I lifted the bottle to my lips but Jack tapped me on the arm.

'Me first,' he said.

I looked at him for a second and then shrugged. It was only fair. After all, he had risked his butt when he nicked the beers from Pete. I passed the bottle over and he took a long drink.

'Jack!' Mrs Johnson exclaimed from the doorway.

I thought she was going to drop dead on the spot but she just stood there, her mouth open, showing the ground-down stubs of her teeth. She looked at each of us in turn and, then, she ripped into *me*, ranting and raving as she waved her flabby arms in the air, and blamed me for leading the others astray, even though Jack was the one guzzling out of the beer bottle when she shuffled through the door.

Well, I'd had enough of her and I didn't care if she was a fucking living treasure, I was going to tell her just where she could get off.

But Jack stepped in first. 'Hey, Mrs Johnson,' he said, getting to his feet. He wiped beer from his chin and handed Danny the bottle. 'Did we frighten you?' As he talked, he guided her away from the shed and back towards her house, using all his charm to calm her down and smooth things over.

'You'd better take Danny home,' I told Alyce.

'What are you going to do?' she asked, as they jumped the back fence into the lane.

'I'm going to see what the nosy old cow has to say.' I waved her off and followed Jack up to Mrs Johnson's house, where I stood under her kitchen window, listening.

I could hear water running into a kettle and the clink of cups as Jack started making her some tea, all the time talking to her, reassuring her that it was the first time that we had ever done anything like that.

'Alcohol is the devil's poison, Jack,' she warned.

'I know, Mrs Johnson. We were just experimenting. Didn't you ever experiment when you were young?' Jack asked, innocent as new snow.

'Yes, I guess I did, but I was much older than you. You're only twelve.'

'Nearly thirteen.'

'Oh, right. I guess that makes all the difference,' said Mrs Johnson. She slurped noisily at her tea.

'Kids try things a bit younger these days,' Jack said.

Mrs Johnson sniffed. 'Maybe so. But in your case, I think it's that sister of yours,' she said, as I knew she eventually would. 'She's a bad influence on you, Jack. If you let her, she'll be the ruin of you.'

'Aw, Mira's okay, Mrs Johnson.'

'I don't think so,' she replied. A chair scraped and I heard her shuffling across the floor. When she spoke again, she was directly above me. 'I'm going to have to tell your parents about what was going on to-night, Jack, for your own sake. I couldn't have it on my conscience if a lovely boy like you went down one of life's darker paths.'

'But, Mrs Johnson—'

I didn't wait to hear any more. Jack was usually pretty good at sweet talking adults, but if he couldn't convince Mrs Johnson not to tell Mum and Dad what we were doing, we'd be in a shitload of trouble - well, maybe not Jack so much, but definitely me - and the old bag sounded determined to spill her guts. That would screw up my life in all sorts of ways.

I'd worked hard to convince my parents that I was a 'good girl' who was a responsible and positive role model for her younger brother. I kept my grades up (having the smartest girl in school as a best friend helped) and avoided trouble where I could. When I couldn't avoid trouble, I made sure that whatever went down happened under my parents' radar. I didn't complain (too much) when they wanted me to work in our pharmacy and I did the jobs around the house that no one else wanted to do, like cleaning out the bins or picking up the dog shit from the nature strip out the front of our house. I hated it - the good girl crap - but it was part of my plan to get out of the Bay.

I'd talked Mum into letting me go to Canberra with Jack, if he got a scholarship with the AIS, so he'd have some family support. What I didn't tell her was, after Jack was settled, I'd be on the first bus to Sydney and the opportunities for fame and fortune that I knew were waiting for me there.

But, if Mrs Johnson blabbed to my parents, especially about something like this, they'd change their minds about me and then my plans would be screwed for sure. I'd end up working in our pharmacy (like Dad wanted) for the rest of my miserable, ordinary, unglamorous life.

I jogged across the street and up our driveway. My bedroom was at the back of the house and I'd arranged things so that I could get in and out of my room whenever I wanted without disturbing my parents. I slipped quietly through my window - there was no point in being stupid - and got comfortable on my bed before taking out my phone. I had to talk to Alyce so we could come up with a believable cover story before morning.

My message was brief: *CM now!*

As I hit 'send', my phone chimed an alert and I jumped. *Shit*, I thought, pressing it to my chest while I held my breath and strained to hear movement in the house, but there were only the usual afternoon sounds: the groan of settling timber, cricket on the TV, the clunk of pipes in the bathroom, the hum of mum's old Singer, Dad's armchair spectating — *Catch it, ya mug!*

Yep, normal-ville at the Falling residence.

I released the air in my lungs and looked at my phone, expecting a text from Alyce with some lame excuse for why she couldn't call me right this second. Instead, there was an email notification.

Oh crap.

There was only one reason Alyce would email me; her parents had confiscated her phone again, which meant they'd caught her out on something, and the only thing Miss Goodie-two-shoes had been up to lately was our little adventure in Mrs Johnson's shed. 'I bet Danny blabbed,' I said aloud, listening for commotion in the house again. Nothing. I clicked the icon to open the email, thinking, *I bloody kill him if he's*— but the message was from someone called Saucy Jack.

At first, I thought another sleaze-ball was getting his rocks off by sending me porn. But there was nothing about sex toys or erotic videos, just some crazy stuff about secrets and blood. It was weird, although the bit about being a star did make me smile.

I figured it was probably from Jack. He was always sending me crap off the Net or emailing me for the most stupid reasons. It was his way of annoying me and he was really good at it because, right then, I felt like strangling him!

I clicked on the reply button and composed a little note telling Jack exactly where he could stick his email. I was about to hit the send button when he climbed through my window. He was sweating and his breath came in quick pants, as if he'd just run the hundred metres.

'She's gonna tell them,' he said, slumping down beside my bed.

'What happened, Muffin-boy?' I said, forgetting the email for the moment. 'You were supposed to convince her to keep her mouth shut.'

'It's not my fault. I tried to talk her out of telling, but—' he trailed off.

'But what?' There was always 'but' when Jack was supposed to take care of something.

'She doesn't like you,' Jack said, smirking. 'She thinks you are leading me astray.'

'What a load of bullshit!' I seethed. 'Didn't the senile old bitch see you sucking on that beer bottle tonight?'

Jack shook his head. 'Forget Mrs Johnson. What are we going to do about Mum and Dad?'

I took a few deep breaths and let them out slowly (a trick I learned from Mum's yoga videos) while I thought about the problem. 'Nothing,' I said, with a shrug. 'If she's gonna put us in, we'll just have to deal with it.' I turned my phone towards him. 'Listen, did you send me this?'

Jack read the message on the screen. 'Nope. Must be from one of your weirdo boyfriends.'

'Shut up! Are you sure you didn't send it?'

'Are you losing your hearing?'

'Well, who's it from then?'

'How would I know?' Jack replied, reading the email again. He thought for a moment and then nodded, 'Jack the Ripper sometimes called himself Saucy Jack in his letters to the newspaper.'

'Really? How do you know that?'

He looked at me as though I was mentally defective. 'Ever heard of the Net?' he asked, and winced when I pinched his arm.

'So what are you saying? That Jack the Ripper sent me an email?'

Jack wasn't impressed. 'No, just that it's probably from some freak *pretending* to be Jack the Ripper.'

'I guess you're right. But don't you think it's a bit personal? I mean, it's addressed to 'Falling Star' and our last name is Falling, and we both know I'm going to be a star.' I flashed him a dazzling smile.

'Just a coincidence,' Jack said, moving towards

my window. 'Anyway, you should be more worried about us getting busted.'

I looked at my brother and wondered if he was telling the truth. I wasn't completely convinced that he hadn't sent me the email, but I decided to let it go. 'Don't sweat it, Jack. If we can't get around Mum and Dad, we'll just have to suffer whatever punishment they give us. It won't be for long, probably a month, maybe less.'

Jack groaned and I knew he was thinking about the extra training sessions he'd have to get through.

'And, you never know, maybe old Mrs Johnson will change her mind.'

'Or die in her sleep,' Jack muttered.

I laughed. 'Huh, we're not that lucky! Now get out of my room. I want to work out who sent me this email.'

Not long after, I heard him open the front door and call out to our parents. Then, it was my turn to make a big entrance, which was a stupid but necessary part of the game.

Mum wanted to chat and, since she probably wouldn't be feeling so talkative tomorrow, I curled up beside her on the lounge. She did most of the talking though, because I was thinking about the email.

'Mira, are you listening?'

'What? Oh, sorry, Mum. I've got a bit of a headache. I think I might go to bed, okay?'

'Are you all right?' she asked.

'Sure. Too much sun, that's all,' I said, giving her a quick hug. 'Night, Dad. Night, Jack.'

For the next half an hour, I tried to find out who'd sent me the email, but none of my on-line friends knew anything about it and every message I sent in reply came straight back, marked as undeliverable.

As I sat reading through the message for the hundredth time, I remembered the email I'd received the year before from N.K. Could this be from the same person? I hunted through my email and brought up the message. The address was across the top of the page: nkelly@thegretamob.com.

There was something familiar about the address and I racked my brains trying to figure out what it was. Then, suddenly it hit me - nkelly (and N.K.) stood for Ned Kelly, Australia's most famous bushranger.

Well, that's just great, I thought. *If Jack is telling the truth, then someone posing as two notorious murderers has been sending me emails. God, didn't people have anything better to do with their lives?*

I clicked on the 'new mail' button and typed in the nkelly address. The note I composed was short and to the point: *Quit sending me emails, dead shit, or else.* I hit 'send' and waited for a reply.

A part of me still thought Jack was behind the emails. It was stupid to think that it could be anyone else, and completely insane to think that the messages actually came from Ned Kelly or Jack the Ripper. What were they doing, emailing unsuspecting mortals from Hell's only Internet cafe? Not likely.

A few seconds after I sent the email, it was spat back at me with an 'unknown domain' message. I sighed in frustration and decided to leave working out who it was from until the morning - assuming that I was still alive after my parents got through with me.

But, as it turned out, I wasn't the one who was dead the next morning.

FOUR

Like every other Saturday, Mum woke me with a knock on my door. I rolled over, looked at my clock - 6:40 a.m. - and groaned.

'Go away, it's too early to get yelled at,' I muttered, burrowing beneath my pillow.

Mum knocked again, louder.

That's weird, I thought. Usually when the shit hit the fan, Mum would knock once and then barge straight in, laying down the law like Moses with the Ten Commandments.

'I'm awake,' I called, lifting my pillow.

The door opened with a gentle snick and I peeked out, expecting to see the face of damnation. Instead, Mum was pale and tears were slipping down her cheeks. I sat up, suddenly afraid.

'What is it?' I asked.

She walked over and sat on my bed, the soft roundness of her hip moulding into my thigh. 'Mira, I have some terrible news. Mrs Johnson is dead.'

I stared at her for a moment, wondering what I should say. Tears filled my eyes and she pulled me into her arms and rocked me gently, as though I was still a baby. I let her hold me for a little while and then I got out of bed and walked over to the window. I needed to feel the fresh air against my face. I pushed the window up and leaned on the sill.

'How did it happen?'

'We don't need to go into that.'

'Mum, tell me,' I said, looking over my shoulder.

'But it's all just speculation. Until the police confirm the details—'

'Mum!'

For a moment I thought she would continue to hold out, then she said, 'Okay, if you must know. The talk is that she was doing some early morning baking, whipping up a batch of those chocolate muffins that everyone loves, when someone broke into her house and attacked her.'

'And?'

Mum gave an exasperated sigh. 'They're saying someone crept up behind her - you know how hard of hearing she is was - and hit the poor dear over the head with one of those heavy, old-fashioned muffin trays she uses.' Her voice caught and she cleared her throat. 'It was still hot. There was a burn mark on the side of her face.' She hesitated again. 'Then, she fell and hit her head on the corner of the oven.'

'Is that what killed her?'

'Probably,' Mum said.

'What do you mean *probably*?' She pressed her lips together, as though she was trying to stop the words from coming. 'C'mon, Mum. If you don't tell me, someone else in town will.'

She looked at me grimly, knowing I was right. 'Fine. The ambulance officers found a chocolate muffin in her mouth. They think her attacker stuffed it down her throat until she choked. Satisfied?'

I shrugged. 'Have you told Jack yet?'

'Dad's with him now.' She rubbed her hands across her face and sighed again. 'I'd better check on them. Will you be all right?'

'Sure, I just need some time, you know, to absorb it,' I said.

She tried to smile and failed. 'Time heals all wounds, Mira. Your grandma used to say that, you know,' she said, as she opened my door and stepped into the hallway.

I stayed at the window for a long time, listening to the sounds of the house; the hollow clump of feet on the wooden floors; the rattle of the glass panels in the front door; the squeal of hinges in the bathroom and, always, the voices.

It was weird, but I'd never realised how popular and respected my parents were until Mrs Johnson pulled the pin. I guess it was because they owned the pharmacy and knew almost everyone in town, from the newest baby to the oldest geriatric. Then again, maybe it was just that we lived right across the road from the old girl.

Whatever it was, our house had been transformed into the hottest venue in the Bay, drawing the curious and the grieving. They crowded onto our front veranda like seagulls scrounging a free lunch, and watched the police and ambulance officers as they tramped in and out of Mrs Johnson's house.

By mid-afternoon, the carnival had begun to quieten down and Jack appeared at my door. He looked tired and gloomy. 'Isn't it awful, Mira?' he said. 'I was just talking to her last night and then, wham, she's gone.'

'Yeah. It makes you realise how vulnerable you

are, doesn't it?'

'I suppose so.' Jack was staring at the floor, his curly hair hiding his eyes. 'I guess this means we're out of trouble.'

I crossed the bedroom and stood in front of him. 'It looks that way. Hey, maybe we got lucky, after all,' I said, brushing the hair away from his face.

He shook it back into place and said, 'Still, it's kinda weird.'

'What?'

'Well, don't you think it's a bit strange that she was murdered the night before she was going to rat us out?'

I shook my head. 'Not really. Shit happens, you know. It's like a guy who turns left instead of right and misses the ten-car pile-up that kills everyone except the woman who decided to let her husband drive. It's fate, that's all. Mrs Johnson would've been dead this morning whether she was going to tell on us or not.'

'Right. Fate,' Jack said, doubtfully. He was quiet for a moment and then he looked straight at me for the first time. 'You didn't have anything to do with what happened to her?'

'Did *you*, Jack?' I asked, arching my eyebrows.

'Hell no! How could you say that?' he spluttered, his eyes wide and innocent.

'Exactly, how could you say something like that?' I demanded, grabbing his arm and yanking him towards me until our faces were almost touching. 'It was just fate, Jack. Don't make it into anything more than that.'

'Okay, Mira,' he said, pulling free.

He turned away and scurried along the hallway to his room. As he passed through the doorway, he glanced back and I thought I saw, just for an instant, the flicker of a smile, but it was gone so quickly that I couldn't be sure.

Jack and I never spoke about what happened to Mrs Johnson again. We went on as though nothing had changed. We bickered over the TV and the bathroom; borrowed stuff from each other without asking (more bickering); and covered each other's butt when we got up to no good. But no matter how normal things seemed, there was always something between us; festering like an abscess, until it finally burst on the day that Danny decided to race Lilly Holborn.

FIVE

The Johnson house stood empty for three years, even though a small army of tradespeople regularly worked on the property, painting, roofing and tidying up the gardens until it didn't look half-bad. Still, no one seemed to want to buy the place.

Mum and Dad believed the house stayed empty out of respect for Mrs Johnson, but I thought it was because no one wanted to buy a place where they knew someone had been murdered. I mean, just imagine cooking your Sunday roast in the same oven that Mrs Johnson had smashed her brains out on. It'd be enough to make you puke.

So, it came as a surprise when an interstate removal truck pulled up in front of the house early one morning. We were having breakfast when Mum stood up and went to the window.

'Well, looks like we're finally getting new neighbours,' she said, peering through the curtains.

'It's about time,' Dad said, pushing his chair away from the table. 'I don't like having an empty house in the street. It invites trouble.' He strode towards the window, muttering something about vandals under his breath, but changed direction when the phone started to ring. He looked at Mum and rolled his eyes as he picked up the receiver.

News gets around quickly in a small town and it wasn't long before the Bay was buzzing with gossip. Our phone rang constantly and Mum's friends started 'popping in' for a quick chat (and a gawk). Everyone wanted to know about the new neighbours, but what could we tell them? The removal truck dumped its load of expensive furniture, including the biggest television I'd ever seen, and a guy from a security company installed an alarm. But there was no sign of human inhabitants.

Then, one afternoon as I was sitting on the veranda painting my toenails and studying for the HSC (a girl has to have priorities), an emerald-green four wheel drive - so new that the paint still looked wet - pulled into the driveway across the street. I dropped the brush back into the bottle, pushed aside my science book and scuttled over to the railing, hiding behind the clump of palm trees that grew in our front garden.

After a minute, the driver's door swung open and a tall, middle-aged man got out. He marched around the car and opened the front passenger door. A shadow moved inside the dark interior, like a spider in a hole, and a stick-thin woman emerged into the morning sun. Her hand came up to protect her face and she bolted for the shady entry of the house, as if the sun would melt her.

The man shook his head and slammed the door shut behind her. He stalked down to the back of the car, knocking loudly on the windows as he went past, and yanked open the rear door. I could hear him talking to himself as he pulled suitcase after suitcase out of the car.

'What are you doing?' Jack asked.

I gave a little yelp of surprise and dragged him behind the palms. 'Shhh. The new neighbours have just turned up,' I whispered.

He frowned and said, 'And what? You're spying on them?'

'Not spying. Gathering information,' I replied, peering through the palm fronds.

'Right,' he said, unconvinced. 'Any kids?'

'Don't know yet.'

At that moment, the back doors opened simultaneously and two teenagers stepped out of the car. They were dressed in black, right up to the dark sunglasses that covered their eyes.

'Well, that answers that question,' Jack said.

'Great. We're living across the road from a pair of gothic freaks,' I groaned.

Jack elbowed me in the ribs. 'Aw, come on, they mightn't be that bad.'

'Yeah, you're right,' I said, shoving him away. 'At least they look like *rich* gothic freaks. That's something.'

The new kids walked down the driveway. They scanned the street and spoke briefly to each other. Then, they looked over at our house.

'I think they can see us,' Jack said, stepping out from behind the palms. He raised his hand and waved.

'God, Jack, don't encourage them,' I said, pulling on his arm.

Jack shook off my hand. 'You're weird sometimes,' he said, with a crooked grin. He hooked his backpack over his shoulder and loped down the front steps.

I smiled. 'Where are you going?' I called after him.

'Beach,' he replied, jamming his body board into the rack attached to the back of his bike. 'The swell's good. You should come down.'

I looked down at my half-finished toenails and the stack of textbooks spread out on the table behind me and sighed. 'Maybe later.'

Across the street, the rear door of the car slammed shut and the man picked up some of the suitcases he had stacked on the ground. 'Sebastian! Lilly! Give me a hand with these bags,' he demanded, as he stumbled over the lawn.

The kids stared at us for a moment longer before turning away. As they walked slowly up the driveway and passed the mountain of waiting baggage, they linked hands.

'Oh yeah. *Definitely* weird,' I said, as they disappeared inside the house.

SIX

'What are you going to do?' Alyce said.

It was a question I'd been asking myself all week, ever since Dad had turned into the world's biggest loser and told me that I'd be working full-time in the pharmacy after the holidays.

No Canberra.

No Sydney.

No drama school.

No life.

Swirls of sand drifted around our feet as we made our way through the dunes that separated Harvest Bay from the open ocean. It was the first day of the school holidays and our first day of freedom from the school system that had dominated our lives for the last thirteen years.

It should've been a great day.

The sky was an inverted blue bowl that shimmered with trapped heat. The sand burned beneath our feet, making us dance between the spinifex and saltbush, desperate for a small slice of shade. From beyond the dunes, came the rhythmic pounding of the surf and the taste of salt in the morning air.

But my dad - the bastard - had ruined the day's promise with his unbelievable decision to end my search for fame before it even started.

'Hello? What are you going to do?' Alyce repeated.

'I don't know yet, but I have to find a way out of here. I can't be stuck in the Bay for the rest of my life.'

Alyce made a disapproving sound in the back of her throat. 'You shouldn't have slacked off at school.'

'Hey, it wasn't like I was flunking out or anything,' I said, defensively.

'No, but you were an A student and then you started getting Cs. What did you expect your parents to do?'

'There's more to life than getting A's in science, you know. Besides, some of the biggest stars never even finished school. Kylie Minogue left school at seventeen and look where she is now.'

Alyce rolled her eyes (she'd heard this argument before). 'But Kylie had a lot of talent to begin with.'

I stopped and looked at her. '*I've* got a lot of talent too.'

Alyce wrapped her arm around my shoulders and hugged me briefly. 'Yeah, I know you do,' she said, as we started walking again. 'And I know you work hard in those acting classes you take. By the way, have you told your mum and dad about them yet?'

I shook my head. 'I paid for them with my money, so it's none of their business.'

Alyce looked at me for a second and then shrugged. 'Anyway, Kylie's been singing and acting since she was like ten or something. You've been in a couple of school plays.'

'Everyone has to start somewhere,' I muttered.

'I know. All I'm saying is I think you have to be

a bit realistic.'

'God! You sound just like my dad,' I said, disgusted. 'Next you'll be saying "Working in the pharmacy will give you a good foundation for the future. And if you study hard at TAFE..." blah, fucking, blah.' I looked at her through slitted eyes. 'It's not happening, Alyce.'

'Well, then, you'd better come up with an idea pretty quick,' she said, as we topped the final dune.

I took a deep, shaky breath and forced my anger back into its box. 'Don't worry,' I said, scanning the white ribbon of beach below us. 'I'm already working on a new plan.'

As always, the shore was sharply divided. To the south, the brightly coloured towels and umbrellas of the summer tourists dotted the sand. To the north, the town kids hung out in loose, shifting groups, sunbaking, surfing, flirting and ignoring the interlopers at the other end of the beach. Except if they were cute and had the guts to cross the no-man's land between us and them.

A lone figure stood in this empty section of beach, staring out to sea, one arm supporting a surfboard.

'Look,' I said, nudging Alyce. 'There's the chick who moved in across the road from us.'

I'd seen my new neighbours a few times since they'd rocked up to the Johnson's place - mostly getting in and out of the car, and once I'd caught the boy watching me as I went out to the mailbox - but I'd been too busy with my frigging HSC and celebrating the end of school (so many parties, so little time) to go over and introduce myself. My original idea about them hadn't changed; I still thought they were freaks but the guy was sort of cute too, in a dark, the-world-hates-me-so-fuck-the-world kind of way.

'So, what's she like?' Alyce asked, shading her eyes against the sun.

I lifted a shoulder and feigned indifference. 'I don't know,' I said, glancing down the beach to where a fat woman in a bright red cozzie was wrestling a podgy toddler into a sun shirt, their flesh pig-pink in the bright sun. I shuddered and looked back to the girl on the sand.

'I haven't had a chance to talk to her yet. But Jack saw her and her brother at the skate ramps on the weekend. He reckons they're pretty cool. Did you know they're twins? Not identical, just born at the same time. Her name's Lilly— Lilly Holborn.'

'Lilly?' Alyce said, curling her lip.

I sniggered. 'I know. What were her parents thinking? Her brother was luckier. His name is Sebastian.'

'I suppose that's not too weird, although it sounds a bit stuck-up.'

'Really? I like it. It's a good, strong name,' I remarked. Alyce glanced at me as I led the way down the face of the dune and I quickly changed the subject before she could get too curious. 'I'll tell you something that is weird. They already knew about Jack even before he talked to them.'

'How?'

'Sally Millar,' I said. 'Jack's old running buddy, remember?'

'The one with the dead rabbit?'

I nodded. 'Sally met the twins at that special athletics school in Brisbane that she went to and, when their parents decided to move to the Bay, she told them to look Jack up.' I pointed to a spot on the sand a few metres behind Lilly, who was now sitting on her board, watching a solitary surfer among the waves. 'Here okay?'

'Sure.'

We dropped our stuff in a pile and while we set up our towels and put on sunscreen, I said, 'Jack messaged Sally to get the goss on them, and guess what? They're loaded!'

'So?'

'So rich people always know famous people,' I explained.

Alyce stopped rubbing lotion into her shoulder and a puzzled expression crossed her face. 'What do you think they're doing here, Mira? I mean, if you were rich and knew a lot of famous people, would you move to a place like Harvest Bay?'

I squirted sunscreen into my hand and motioned for her to turn around. 'No way. If I was rich I'd probably move to Hollywood or Monte Carlo, or some other place where people with money hang out,' I said, rubbing the lotion into her back. When it had disappeared into her skin, I turned around and Alyce returned the favour.

'That's what I mean. Why the hell would anyone choose to move here?'

'Well, Sally told Jack that there was some sort of trouble in the family. Who knows, maybe she's pregnant or something?' I suggested, inclining my head towards Lilly. I cut my eyes back to Alyce. 'And maybe they need someone to help them out?'

Alyce folded her arms across her chest and thrust her hip forward. It was the stance she used when she was 'mothering' Danny. She raised her eyebrows and

51

her voice deepened slightly, all without her realising. 'Are these people part of your new plan, Mira?'

'Maybe,' I said, as I adjusted my bikini top.

Alyce groaned. 'God, why can't you just run away from home like a normal person?'

I wrapped my arm around her shoulder. 'What would be the point of that? My face on a police noticeboard isn't going to make me famous. But, if I hang out with people who know the right people, then you never know what could happen.'

'So, what are you going to do? Crash their lives like you'd crash a party. They mightn't want you hanging out with them, did you think of that?' Alyce said, shrugging me off and fussily arranging her hair beneath her sun hat.

I smiled and yanked the brim over her eyes. 'Don't worry, Alyce. They'll love me, you wait and see. Now, let's go and say hi.'

Lilly was as still as a statue, only her short, chestnut-coloured hair stirred in the breeze. We stepped around her board and stood in front of her, our shadows falling across her face as she looked up.

'Hi, I'm Mira,' I said, in my friendliest voice.

She was wearing a pair of blue-tinted sunglasses that hid her eyes, but I felt the coldness of her stare anyway. She sighed and shifted on the board so she could watch the ocean again.

I looked at Alyce, who raised a quizzical eyebrow and shrugged. 'Your family moved in across the street from me,' I said, trying a different approach. 'I'm Jack's sister and this is Alyce.'

This time Lilly smiled, revealing small, very white teeth. I smiled back.

She stood up in one graceful movement, as

though her bones were liquid, and straightened the white sarong that was tied loosely across her narrow hips. Her gold belly ring flashed in the sun and the sarong flapped around her legs. I noticed that she had a circle of interlocking black roses tattooed around her ankle.

'Wow, I love your tattoo,' I said, as she bent down and picked up the beach towel lying beside her surfboard.

'Yeah, Sis, it's very sexy.'

I turned towards the voice and felt my skin tighten across my body; the gothic freak had transformed into a golden surfie boy and suddenly I found it hard to breathe. Our eyes locked and, for one long moment, it was as if there was just Sebastian and me on the beach. Then he smiled, just as his sister reached up to kiss him.

'Have you made some new friends, Lilly?' he asked, accepting her kiss before gently pushing her away. He rubbed the towel she gave him through his hair and across his face.

'No,' she said, keeping her back to us.

Sebastian hung the towel around his neck and looked me slowly up and down, his eyes resting at my hips and breasts.

'Hello!' I said, waving my hand in front of his eyes.

He grinned and said, 'You must be Jack's sister. Mira, right?'

'That's what I was just telling her,' I said, pointing towards Lilly.

'Oh, I'm sorry, was that you talking? I couldn't hear you over the squawking of the little kids,' Lilly remarked.

'What?'

'Are you deaf as well as stupid?' Lilly said, slipping off her sunnies. Her eyes were the same colour as Sebastian's, a deep chocolate brown, and they glittered with spite.

'What's your problem?' I demanded, my temper flaring.

Alyce stepped between us and spoke to Sebastian. 'Hi, I'm Alyce.'

'Great, dumb and dumber,' Lilly muttered, as she stalked down to the water's edge.

'Hey!' Alyce exclaimed, taking a step after her.

Sebastian touched her arm. 'Let her go. She hates it here and she's taking it out on everyone around her.'

'*Everyone* hates being in the Bay. That doesn't give her the right to take it out on us. Who does she think she is, anyway? The fucking Queen or something?' I said.

Alyce covered my mouth with her hand. 'What about you? You don't seem to hate being here,' she said as I pushed her hand away.

'What's to hate? There's the beach and the surf. And as long as I don't have to see my parents too often, life's sweet.' He turned towards me and butterflies fluttered in my stomach until he said, 'Where's Jack?'

~

Great, I thought, *I'm standing here in my bikini, talking to the cutest guy on the planet, and all he wants to know about is my brother.* 'He's at a running comp, somewhere out west,' I said, pretending to look at something interesting at the other end of the beach.

'Ah. Okay. I guess I'll catch him some other time.'

'Hey, Romeo, when you're finished with those country slags, can we go?'

'Man, she really is asking for it,' I fumed.

Sebastian laughed and started gathering up their stuff. 'I'll see you girls around.'

Lilly stomped back up the beach, grabbed her board and started dragging it towards the break in the dunes.

'See you later, Lilly,' I called after her. She didn't bother to answer, but shot one manicured finger into the air as she followed Sebastian across the sand.

'Well, isn't she a peach?' I said as they disappeared between the dunes.

'Oh, I don't know. Maybe she'll be all right once we get to know her,' Alyce said, lying down on her towel.

I stared at her, wondering if the sun had softened her brain. 'You're not serious?'

She twisted around and looked up at me. 'You shouldn't always judge people by your first impressions,' she said. 'Besides, if you get in good with Lilly, she might help you hook up with Sebastian.'

'What are you talking about?'

Alyce laughed. 'I saw the way you looked at him.'

'Shut up!' I said, kicking sand at her. 'I'm going for a swim. Are you coming?'

Alyce jumped up and we raced down to the surf, leaving thoughts of the twins behind.

SEVEN

Alyce was totally wrong about Lilly.

She was a complete bitch and nothing we did changed that fact. The only person she was nice to was Jack, but that didn't mean anything because everyone was nice to Jack; after all, he was the kid with the potential to put Harvest Bay on the map. To the rest of us, Lilly was as nasty as a bloodstain a white dress, and the closer I got to Sebastian, the more she hated me.

I guess it was because they were twins.

They were really close when they moved to the Bay - much too close for a normal brother and sister, I thought - and they'd do creepy stuff like finishing each other's sentences and synchronising their movements. Then there was all the kissing and touching.

It was weird. It was gross, and it made me want to rip out her fucking heart. At least until Sebastian explained how things had been for them when they were growing up.

We were sitting outside Parish Pizzeria - *Pizza so good, it's heavenly* - munching on a super supreme and drinking Cokes, when Sebastian said, 'You don't like my sister, do you?'

'Is it that obvious?' I replied, around a mouthful of stringy pizza.

He smiled. 'She's okay, when you get to know her.'

'No. She's definitely not okay. Normal people don't go around kissing their brothers and stuff.'

'Don't you kiss your brother?'

'Sure. Sometimes. At Christmas and on his birth-day. Maybe.' I grimaced at the thought. 'But I don't hang all over him the way Lilly hangs over you. What the hell is *that*, anyway?'

'We're just close,' Sebastian mumbled.

'Nah-ah. Alyce and Danny, they're close. But you and your freaky sister, that's something else completely.'

Sebastian frowned and said, 'Don't talk about Lilly like that. You don't know what our lives have been like. You look at us and see two rich kids whose parents give them anything they want. But they never gave us what we really needed—' He fell silent as though he couldn't bring himself to finish the thought, then he shrugged, 'They just fucking ignored us,' he said.

It was my turn to frown. 'Lots of kids grow up without getting any attention from their parents, but they don't carry on like you and Lilly.'

He shrugged. 'Look, who gives a crap what Lilly and I do? It's not a big deal. We just like to screw with people's minds, you know. It's a shock tactic, that's all.' He dropped his half-eaten slice of pizza onto the tray and looked across the street.

On the boat ramp beside the pub, two fishermen were cleaning their catch, long-bladed knives flashing in the sunlight, while their kids scooped up handfuls of fish guts and threw them, with shrieks of delight, to the squabbling, bucket-mouthed pelicans.

'When we were kids, Mum and Dad were almost never at home. He was always out of town on business. She had her charity work. And when they were home, he'd be slinging down whisky as though prohibition was about to be re-introduced and she'd be shit-faced on Valium,' Sebastian said, watching the kids.

'That must have been tough,' I remarked, although I really thought it'd be a relief to have parents who ignored you most of the time.

He finished his Coke. 'We started doing stuff to shock them, just so they'd look at us, you know. But it's hard to shock someone who doesn't even know what planet they're on and, after a while, it sank in that we just had each other. Now we do stuff just to piss them off.'

I was quiet for a minute, thinking about what he'd told me. 'Is that why you moved to the Bay, because your parents had... problems?' I kept my idea about Lilly being pregnant to myself.

'That was part of it. But there was also his job and the other women. Mum just cracked up one day and it was move here or get a divorce.' Sebastian snorted. 'I guess they're giving it one more try.' He stared moodily at the ground between his Nikes and I searched for something to say that would cheer him up.

'So, does it work?' I asked, finally.
'What?'
'That stuff that you do with Lilly.'
'Yeah. They go bugshit.' Sebastian laughed. It

was an ugly sound, like a phlegm-filled cough. He picked a piece of pineapple off the pizza and mashed it between his fingers. 'One of these days, all the booze and dope will catch up with them - or else we'll shock them into a heart attack - and then Lilly and I will be free to do what we want.' He flicked the pineapple away.

'Um, wouldn't it be easier and quicker to take them out with a baseball bat or something?' I joked.

His brow creased as if he was seriously considering my suggestion, then he smiled. 'Can't. It'd blow our inheritance.'

'Oh well, we can't have that!' I took another slice of pizza and ate while I thought about the question that had been bugging me since the day we met on the beach. 'Have you and Lilly ever… you know?' I hesitated, feeling blood seep into my cheeks and I looked up at Sebastian, hoping he'd fill in the blanks. But he just sat across from me with an amused look on his face. The bastard was going to force me to finish the question. I took a sip from my Coke and then spat out the words.

'Have you and Lilly slept together?'

'Sure,' he said, casually twirling the ice in his glass.

My mouth dropped open.

'When we were five.'

'Oh,' I said, sitting back in my chair. My face burned and I couldn't seem to drag my eyes away from my fingernails.

Sebastian leaned across the table, his face serious. He grabbed my hands and squeezed them, hard. 'Lilly and I do some weird shit sometimes, Mira, but we're not sick.'

'I know that,' I said, quickly. 'Look, I'm sorry, it was a stupid thing to ask. It's just that you're so… close.'

'Yeah, we're close, but everything we do is for shock value. It doesn't mean anything, okay?'

'Ah-huh, okay,' I replied, as he released my hands.

He picked up the last slice of pizza and offered it to me. I shook my head and watched as he tore into it. I waited until he'd finished eating, then I said, 'So, what's the most shocking thing you've ever done?'

He scratched his cheek. 'Playing tongue hockey with Lilly in front of the Lord Mayor of Brisbane at his annual charity gala.'

'God, that's disgusting,' I groaned.

'Yeah, and it really pissed off our parents.'

'I bet,' I said, reaching across the table. 'You know, if you and me are going to be together, you can't do stuff like that anymore. I don't want a boyfriend who even *thinks* about kissing his sister.'

He raised his eyebrows and a wicked smirk surfaced on his face. 'Is that what I am? Your boyfriend?'

'Whatever,' I said, shaking my head, 'I'm serious, though. There can't be any more of that crap.'

'I know, but it's hard to give up something you've been doing for so long. In some strange way, it makes me feel closer to Lilly, more a part of her.' He chewed at his lip as he searched for the words to explain. 'You're not a twin, so you probably won't understand.'

'I have a brother,' I offered.

'Not the same.'

'Maybe not, but I understand that you have to be your own person and you can only do that by ditching Lilly. Tell her to live her own life.'

He was quiet for a long minute and then he looked into my eyes. 'Lilly who?' he asked.

It was the perfect answer. And he was the perfect guy: cute, rich, connected and, best of all, in love with me. The only real problem was Lilly.

EIGHT

If I'd learnt anything from listening to Dad coach Jack over the years, it was the value of psychological warfare. Dad was a firm believer in sledging the competition, in undermining their confidence, and disrupting their preparation - anything that would give Jack the edge over his opponents. Not that Jack went in for that. He always tried to win fairly but that didn't stop Dad giving him the 'pep talk' before he took to the track.

'I want you to forget about all that fair play and good sportsmanship crap they teach you at school, son. Whoever said, 'It's not winning that counts but how you play the game' never took the gold. Winning is everything and second place is just a pretty way of saying 'loser'. Doors open for winners, Jack. You keep that in mind and do whatever it takes to get across that line first. Understand?'

Jack would nod enthusiastically, and then go out and run his own race, most of which he - thankfully - won.

Dad mightn't have reached Jack with his whacked-out philosophy for getting what you want in life, but I heard him loud and clear. So when it came to taking care of Lilly, I knew exactly what I had to do.

The renovations on the Johnson house began about a month after the Holborn's moved in. One morning our usually quiet street was crowded with vans and utes, a mini-skip and a small army of workmen, who scurried over the house like ants before a storm.

Rolls of threadbare carpet and reams of faded wallpaper were carried from the house, while lino tiles from the kitchen floor sailed through the space where the window used to be. The toilet that I had spent so many Saturdays cleaning was dumped unceremoniously into the mini-skip, along with the front door that Jack had taken a whole weekend to paint. It was a little sad, somehow, like watching Mrs Johnson die all over again.

Mum and I were on the veranda a few afternoons later, sipping iced tea and eating our lunch as we watched the work progress and chatted about what we thought the Holborn's might do to the house.

'They're going to leave the outside pretty much the way it is to preserve the look of the neighbourhood,' Mum informed me between the crashing and banging.

'Great, there's nothing like living beside a crapcoloured house to make you feel good about your life,' I said, swallowing the last of my tea.

'Enough of the language, Mira,' Mum said, absently. She was watching a plumber, who was kind of cute if you liked guys over twenty-five, carrying a new stainless steel sink into the house. 'Anyway, once the bricks have been pressure cleaned, I think you'll find they're more of a reddish-brown.'

'Whatever. So how did you come by this information?'

'Clare told me.'

'*Clare* told you? I asked, raising my eyebrows.

'Yes. She came into the pharmacy for something the other day.'

'What?' I asked, with a mischievous grin. 'Worming tablets? Anti-fungal cream? Laxatives?'

Mum slapped me playfully on the arm and said, 'That's none of your business.' She placed her cup on a tray in the middle of the table and stood up. 'Could you take that inside for me, Mira?'

'Sure, but where are you going?'

'Oh, I thought I'd pop over and see what Clare thinks of the renovations so far,' Mum replied, nodding across the street.

'Well, hang on a second and I'll come with you,' I said, quickly taking the tray into the house.

I'd been waiting for an opportunity to meet Sebastian's parents. I wanted to see if they were as bad as he made them out to be. After talking to my mum, who was usually pretty good at working out what people were about, I thought maybe he'd been exaggerating just to get on my good side, which for him, was probably somewhere south of my collarbones!

We strolled across the street, skirting piles of rubbish and mounds of dirt from the freshly turned garden. The place looked like the set of a reality TV show before the miraculous transformation and I kept expecting a camera to be shoved in my face at any moment. (I smoothed my hair down and smiled broadly, just in case.)

Inside, the house wasn't much better. There was crap everywhere: ladders, drop sheets, scaffolding, and tins of paint by the dozen. Still, I was surprised by how much the place had changed in a few short days. Before Mrs Johnson took the express elevator to heaven, the house had been dark and dreary, and filled with an overpowering piss-in-the-corner stench that always made me gag. Now, light poured in and all I could smell was the fresh paint that was being slapped onto the walls.

I followed Mum into the kitchen where we found Clare Holborn standing in the middle of a group of large workmen. She seemed even thinner than when I'd first seen her dashing across the front lawn, and sort of fragile like a daisy growing among boulders. She wasn't intimidated by the men, though, and they listened closely as she gave them precise instructions in her clipped, no-nonsense voice.

Maybe it was her face that held their attention.

She was pretty for someone her age - I found out later that she was forty-five, but she looked the same age as my mum who was thirty-eight - but I think what really fascinated them was her money and the class that came with it. She was standing amid a half-demolished house but she could have been standing on a fifty-foot yacht, sipping champagne, and look just as comfortable.

She finished giving her instructions to the workers and as they headed off to do what she asked, she saw Mum and I standing just outside the doorway. 'Susan,' she exclaimed, hurrying over to us. 'I'm sorry about the mess. There is so much that needs to be done to make this place liveable.' She let out a long-suffering sigh.

Mum laughed and made some comment but I had tuned them out. Mrs Johnson died in this kitchen and, even though it didn't look the same any more, in my mind I could still see where everything belonged. I approached the spot where her body had been found, and imagined the blood dripping from the wound in her head, her purple face bulging with chocolate muffin. I shuddered a little and turned back to my mum and Clare.

'But where will you eat tonight?' I heard Mum ask.

'Well, I found an adorable little Italian restaurant on one of my trips into Bridgewater.'

Mum shook her head. 'There's no need to go into Bridgewater for dinner when you can eat with us. We're having a few friends over anyway and it'll be a good opportunity for you to meet some people from town. What do you say?'

'That's very generous, Susan, but I think I would prefer to dine with my family tonight. You understand, don't you?' Before Mum had a chance to respond, Clare turned to me and said, 'You must be Mira. I've been hearing a lot about you from Sebastian.'

'Hello, Mrs Holborn, it's very nice to meet you,' I replied, allowing my eyes to drop shyly towards the floor before I looked up at her and smiled. 'You've done an amazing job with the house. I can't believe it's the same place, and everything is coming along so quickly.'

Clare laughed. 'That's what money buys, my dear, efficiency and the right to instantly dismiss whoever isn't pulling their weight.'

'Still, it's a challenge renovating an entire house,' Mum cut in, 'I've always wanted to do something with our place,' she shook her head and moved aside as two workmen carrying a new dishwasher edged into the kitchen, 'but I could never decide where or when I should begin.'

'I don't have that problem,' Clare replied, ushering us into the lounge room to escape the hammering and drilling of the workmen as they installed her new equipment. 'Renovating is a bit of a hobby of mine. I have an agent who looks out for properties on the market that are run-down. I come up with a design and then my team comes in and transforms them into a dream. We usually auction the houses for charity,' she touched her fingers to the still tacky wall and then wiped them on a drop cloth nearby, 'but this one, I think, is a keeper.' As she spoke, she guided us slowly through the house until, almost without realising how we got there, we were standing just inside the front door.

'Well, thank you for coming over but if I don't get back in there, those workmen will start thinking it's time for a break,' Clare said, glancing over her shoulder.

'Yes, if you give a tradesperson an inch, they'll take a mile,' Mum agreed, as if she was the all-knowing guru on such things. 'Well, thank you for the tour and good luck with everything.' She gave Clare a brief hug (it's a small-town thing) and then we headed for home.

At the gate I stopped and said, 'You go ahead, Mum, I just want to ask Mrs Holborn if she knows when Sebastian will be home.'

'Okay, but don't be too long, I may need a hand with dinner.'

I nodded and ran back to the house. I didn't really need to know when Sebastian would be home (he'd gone to the ramps with Jack) but what I did want was a chance to talk to his mum without my mum hanging around. I knocked loudly on the door and Clare looked up from a swatch of carpet samples.

A slight frown crossed her face. 'Did you forget something, Mira?' she asked.

'Sort of. I just wanted to say that if you need any errands done or help around the house maybe some cleaning when the workmen are finished then I'd be more than happy to lend a hand.'

'Thank you, Mira. I'll keep that in mind.' She hesitated and I could see her debating with herself. Then she said, 'You've already been a great help to me.'

I plastered on my warmest smile and inclined my head. 'Really? How?'

'By keeping Lilly and Sebastian company. You and your brother have been a blessing. The twins are finally beginning to act normal...' She broke off, re-alising what she was about to say. She gave her head a little shake and then she patted my arm, 'Well, it's just nice that they've made friends so quickly.'

I shrugged to show that it was no big deal and said, 'They're pretty cool and, you know, fun to hang out with.' That was a joke - Lilly was about as cool as the desert at midday - but it made Clare's eyes sparkle to hear it and I knew I'd made the right impression.

'Well, Mum's expecting me, so I'd better go but remember what I said, anything you need.'

'I'll remember, Mira.'

'Okay, I'll see you around.'

It wasn't until Sebastian came over later in the day that I realised how good an impression I'd made with his mum. I was lying on my bed reading another

Stephen King novel that Alyce had given to me. She'd raved about it - *It's the best book I've ever read. You'll love it!* - but it wasn't doing a whole lot for me. Who cares what an aging arthritic gunslinger, living in some alternate reality, was doing? I sighed and closed the book. My own life was complicated enough.

I stared up at the ceiling, lost in thought, and only slowly became aware that someone was watching me. I looked over at my door and saw Sebastian leaning against the frame.

He smiled at me as he came into the room, 'What were you thinking about?' he wanted to know.

'Nothing important,' I replied, as I sat up and drew my knees towards my chest so he could sit down on my bed. 'How long have you been standing there?'

'Long enough,' he said, in a low, husky voice that made my heart kick up a beat or two and sent a shiver rippling across my skin.

I tried to think of something cool and witty to say in reply but the best I could come up with was, 'So, when did you get back from the ramps?' I groaned inside; seriously lame.

Sebastian didn't seem to notice. 'About an hour ago. Mum wanted to show me some stuff around the house, so I had to have the 'tour' before I could come over.' He took my hand and rubbed my fingers between his own, sending my heart into overdrive. 'Mum said you were over for a visit?'

'Yeah, my mum wanted to stickybeak. Your mum didn't mind, did she?'

'Nope. In fact, she asked me to come over and invite you to dinner with us tonight.'

'Really?'

'Yep. I don't know what you said to her, but you're definitely in her good books. So will you come?'

'Do I look like the kind of girl who would pass up dinner at a swanky restaurant?' I asked, bouncing off the bed. He laughed as I grabbed his hand and led him through the house to the front door.

'We'll pick you up at seven, okay?'

'All right, now get out of here so I can get ready,' I said, as I pushed him towards the stairs.

Seven o'clock came around quickly and I had only just finished with my hair when Sebastian banged on the front door. I raced through the house, yelling goodbye to my family as I ran past the lounge room, and opened the door.

'Wow, you look great,' he said as I stepped onto the veranda.

I'd borrowed Alyce's long black skirt and matched it with a hot pink off-the-shoulder top that accentuated the swell of my breasts without making me look like a slut. Classy and hot, just like the movie stars when they dined out on the town. I was feeling good as we walked down the front path and out to the Holborn's four-wheel drive. Sebastian opened the door for me and I laughed as he pretended to be my valet, holding out his hand to guide me into the car.

My laughter faded when I saw his sister glaring at me from the back seat. 'Oh, hi Lilly,' I said, as I slid across the seat, 'I didn't know you were coming tonight.'

'I wouldn't have if I'd known you were joining us,' she replied sweetly, a shark's grin surfacing on her face.

'What was that, Lilly?' Clare asked from the front of the car.

'Just welcoming our guest, Mother,' Lilly called back, shooting me a disdainful look before she slumped against the chair. She took out a set of head-phones and slipped them over her ears, hit the play button on the iPod beside her and spent the drive into Bridgewater staring out of the window, as if the rest of us didn't exist.

The restaurant was far classier than anything I'd ever been to with Mum and Dad. A fancy dinner for them meant a night at the local fish restaurant or, if they wanted to be really extravagant, at The Happy Dragon, depending on the occasion (birthdays and anniversaries usually qualified) and how much money Dad was willing to spend.

The Olive Garden was tucked away in an arcade near the end of Bridgewater's main street. We parked out the front and, as soon as I got out of the car, I could smell garlic and basil, tomatoes, spicy sausages and the sharp tang of fresh Parmesan cheese. My stomach growled and the Holborn's - except for Lilly, who grimaced with disgust - laughed.

It was crowded in the restaurant, even though it was a Thursday night, and noisy with conversation and laughter. Music poured from a pair of speakers in the ceiling (*La forza del destino* by someone called Verdi, so Clare told me later) and mingled with the clink of glasses and the clatter of pots from the kitchen in a loud and lively mix that made my skin prickle. We made our way through the restaurant and took a table in the back.

When the waitress had collected our order - I was having antipasto, Osso Bucco and hazelnut gelato for dessert - and brought us our drinks, Clare leaned towards me and said, 'I hope your mother didn't mind that we invited you to dinner tonight?'

I smiled and shook my head, 'No, she was fine about it.'

'Are you sure? I know you were having people over.'

'Oh, that was nothing,' I said, waving my hand dismissively. Clare gazed at me with raised eyebrows and I realised she wanted an explanation. I tucked my hair behind an ear. 'Jack won another running competition and my parents are having a few friends over to celebrate. Trust me, it's no big deal, they have one of those dinners almost every weekend. I can afford to miss one.'

'Your brother sounds like a gifted athlete,' said Sebastian's dad, William.

'He's the best in the state, Dad,' Sebastian said. 'His coach thinks he could be faster than Josh Ross.'

'Now that would be impressive,' William said, swirling his glass of red wine. In the light from the candle burning in the middle of our table, it looked like blood, soft and velvety, and I watched it almost mesmerised - not an uncommon state for me when someone started raving about Jack. 'You must be very proud of him, Mira.'

I blinked and looked at William. 'Sorry? Oh, yes, the whole town is proud of Jack, but no one more so than Mum and Dad.' I sighed and took a long sip of my Coke.

'Well, look who's got an inferiority complex,' Lilly quipped, her eyes challenging and malicious.

'Lilly!' Clare said, in a voice strident with reprimand.

'That's enough from you, young lady,' William agreed.

Lilly gave her parents a bored look, but suddenly the tension that had been simmering between her and her parents all evening took on an edge as sharp as sleet.

'It's okay,' I reassured them. 'She's sort of right. I do get a bit sick of the way people go on about my brother, especially my mum and dad.' I shrugged. 'I used to feel resentful until I realised that it was a waste of time. It's just the way things are,' I shot them a smile, 'but that doesn't mean I don't enjoy a night away from all that Jack-worshipping.'

Clare patted my arm and said, 'That decides it then. From now on, there will be no more discussion about Jack.'

The dinner went by swiftly after that. William and Clare mostly ignored us, wrapped in talk of renovations and their latest blue-chip stock acquisition, and I could see a little of what Sebastian had been complaining about, although he didn't seem to mind too much with me there to keep him entertained.

We tried to include Lilly in our conversation, but she stubbornly refused to get involved, except to make the odd snide remark about my taste in clothes or the level of my intelligence. I think she expected me to tell her to piss off (and I really, really wanted to) but I could feel the level of tension rising with each comment so I let it slide. Then, as the dessert was served, the night turned completely sour.

'What are you going to do now that you have finished school, Mira?' Clare asked between bites of her tiramisu.

'Well, I promised my dad that I'd help out in the

pharmacy over the holidays…' I began.

'Good idea,' William interrupted. 'It's always good to get to know the family business. It gives you something to fall back on.' He looked meaningfully at the twins.

'Come on, Dad, don't start,' Sebastian moaned.

'Quite right,' Clare said, nodding at me to continue.

I shifted uncomfortably in my chair. Umm well, next year I'll probably move to Canberra. Mum and Dad are waiting to hear from the Institute of Sport about a scholarship program for Jack and, if he gets in, I'll take up an offer from one of the universities down there.' I didn't tell them about my dad's plans for my future.

'And what will you study?' William asked.

'Mira wants to be an actor,' Sebastian said, squeezing my hand under the table.

Really?' Clare asked as though Sebastian had said I wanted to be the first woman to run naked on Jupiter. 'Do you have to go to university for that?'

'Well, most universities have drama courses, but that's not what I'd be doing. I was thinking about a combined degree in business and science.' I could see the admiration growing in William's eyes. 'But I haven't made up my mind yet.'

'What about acting?' Sebastian asked, frowning.

'Acting is hobby, not a career' I replied, sending him a threatening look. What was he doing? I was trying to get on his parents good side and he was blowing it for me. Everyone knew rich people didn't take actors seriously at least, not until their bank balances were equal to that of a small South American country.

'God, you are so full of crap,' Lilly snapped, drawing the eyes of the diners around us.

'Right, that's it, young lady. I've had enough,' her father said, throwing his napkin on the table. His voice was low and granite hard. 'You have been rude to Mira all evening, while she has borne your malice with admirable restraint. I demand that you apologise to her right this minute and then I don't want to hear another comment from you for the rest of the night.'

Lilly leaned towards him and I thought for a moment that she was going to tell him to fuck off. I could see it in her eyes, flashing like a neon sign, but at the last moment, she controlled herself. Instead, she pointed a shaking finger at me and said, 'Don't you see what she's doing? She's trying to weasel her way into our family. She's already got her hooks into Sebastian and now she's trying to get on your good side by telling you just what you want to hear.'

'Don't be stupid, Lilly. Mira's not trying to do anything,' Sebastian said, coming to my defence.

I covered my smile with my napkin.

Clare gripped Lilly's wrist. 'All I can see is an extremely rude child who's behaving like a spoiled brat,' she said so that only we could hear.

Lilly yanked her arm free and jumped to her feet. She glared at us, her mouth pulled down into a thin angry line. 'Go to hell,' she spat venomously as she turned and strode through the restaurant, ignoring the stares of the other customers.

Her parents and brother were on their feet ready to go after her when I said, 'That's what she wants you to do.'

Clare looked at me and frowned distractedly. 'What?'

I sighed. 'Listen, I'm a teenage girl, right? This is what we do. We throw a tantrum and expect you to come running after us, just like you did when we were little, but by doing that you make it worse next time. It'd be better if we had a coffee or something and gave her some time to cool off. She can't go anywhere. It's an hour back to Harvest Bay, remember.'

'I will not permit her to talk to us like that,' William said.

'If you go out there, you're just going to get into an argument, and that's what she wants. It's her way of getting attention.'

Clare and William sat down again. 'Is that the voice of experience I hear?' Clare asked, looking around for the waitress. When she caught her attention, she ordered four cappuccinos.

I laughed a little and said, 'Sort of. I do have to compete with my extraordinarily talented brother for my parents' attention. But whenever I 'bung one on', as my dad would say, they just ignore me until I get over myself.'

'Maybe I should go and check on her,' Sebastian said.

'No, Mira's right. We are not going to play Lilly's game. We'll have our coffee and, by then, she should have calmed down enough to be reasonable,' Clare said.

When the waitress arrived with the coffee, I leaned into Sebastian and whispered, 'Are you thinking about your sister again?' He looked at me and a flush of colour crept into his cheeks. I squeezed his hand, 'Don't worry. I know bad habits are hard to break. Besides, she'll come round in a minute or two, once she realises that no one's falling for her act.'

'You don't know Lilly,' he said, looking towards the door.

The ride home was pretty awful. William drove the car with grim concentration, while Clare, Sebastian and Lilly stared stubbornly through the windows into the darkness. My efforts at small talk fell on deaf ears and, after a while, I gave up trying to crack the brittle silence that filled the car like a week-old toffee.

Lying in my bed a short time after they'd dropped me off, I had to admit that Lilly probably won the final skirmish of the evening. But then again, judging from the yelling that was coming from her house, I think the battle overall was entirely mine.

NINE

'Mum sent me over to invite you and your family to Christmas lunch,' I said, as I stepped past Clare into the house.

I still couldn't believe it was the same place. What was once dark and mouldering was now bright and breezy, with clean white tiles, pale green walls and sparkling glass everywhere. Huge vases of native flowers - fake but still attractive -provided a splash of colour, while a few paintings and a black and white photograph of the twins hung from the walls. It was tasteful and elegant, just like the house I was going to own one day.

'The house is beautiful, Mrs Holborn.'

'Why thank you, Mira, but I didn't do it on my own,' she squeezed my hand. 'I really appreciate all that you've done over the past few weeks.'

I smiled and waved away her praise. 'As my mum would say, it was the neighbourly thing to do.'

Clare returned my smile and led the way into the kitchen. I sat on one of the high-back barstools lined up along the bench while she poured us a drink of homemade lemonade. It was bloody horrible, like sucking on fresh-cut lemons, but I took a big swig and somehow managed not to grimace or shudder, even though my tongue wanted to shrivel up like a slug doused with salt.

'So will you come for Christmas lunch?' I asked when my mouth had recovered.

Clare shook her head. 'We wouldn't want to impose. After all, Christmas is a time for family.'

'And friends,' I interrupted. I took my glass to the sink, rinsed it and then stacked it in the dishwasher. 'You won't be the only friends there, either, if that's what you're worried about. The Parish's' will be coming over and a few other people from town. And my Aunty Verna will be there too. You'll love her. She's about eighty in the shade and a real crackup.

'She insists on making the Christmas cake every year, but it's so loaded with brandy that no one can eat it. I think she forgets how much she's put in and just keeps adding more until the whole bottle's gone,' I laughed. 'Mum always has to bake a replacement cake and swap it for Aunt Vern's before she can put it on the table. Then, Aunty Vern spends the rest of the day complaining about how the cake needs more brandy.'

'She sounds sweet,' Clare said, smiling.

'She is,' I replied, looking down the hallway as Lilly's bedroom door swung open a centimetre or two. In my mind's eye, I could see her pressing her ear to the gap as she listened in. *What a loser*, I thought, and turned my attention back to Clare. 'So, what do you say? Will you come? Please?'

Clare thought for moment and then said, 'I'll have to check with William to make sure we have no other commitments, but tell your mum that we'd be delighted to come.'

I grinned and clapped my hands. 'Great. It'll be a lot of fun, you'll see.' I started back towards the front door and Clare followed me. 'Thanks for the lemonade,' I said, as Lilly slipped into the lounge room. She shot me an arctic look as she stood against the far wall, arms folded across her chest.

'Hold on a second,' Clare said, as I opened the door. 'What should we bring?'

'Nothing. Mum's got it covered.'

'I have to contribute something, Mira, or I wouldn't feel right.'

'Okay,' I said, holding my hands up in surrender. 'We don't do the traditional Christmas thing. Mum says it's too hot to cook all that stuff, so we usually have prawns, cold chicken, salads, you know, stuff like that.'

'No roasted turkey and cranberry sauce?'

I shook my head.

'Well, my dear, that's just not Christmas.'

At that moment, Lilly pushed off from the wall and sauntered over to us. I watched her approach, feeling a wave of hatred swell inside me, but I covered it with a friendly smile. 'Hello, Lilly,' I said, not expecting a reply and receiving none.

'What's happening with Christmas?' she demanded.

'Manners, Lilly,' Clare replied.

Lilly's eyes searched the roof. 'Sorry, how are you, Mira?' she asked, almost choking on my name.

An image of her rolling around on the floor, tongue sticking out from between her blue-tinged lips, flashed into my mind. 'I'm fine,' I said, turning to Clare, 'so, I'll tell Mum that you're bringing the turkey' - I couldn't help glancing at Lilly - 'and we'll see you on Christmas Day.'

'We'll look forward to it,' Clare said, and even before the door closed, I could hear Lilly yelling.

***

Christmas Day dawned hot and clear. Mum was already in the kitchen when I flopped over on my stomach and slowly let the daylight slip under my eyelids. I lay there for a while, listening to the muffled sounds of platters and pans, the soft clink of punch glasses, the pantry door opening, closing, opening again. For as long as I could remember I had been waking up to those noises; they were as much a part of Christmas morning as the ripping open of carefully wrapped presents.

I looked over at my clock. It was just after seven and I felt the familiar flutter of excitement in my belly as I thought about the presents under the tree in the lounge room. I sniffed deeply, smelling the hint of fresh pine that drifted through our house, and the flutter became a tremor. I threw back my sheet and scrambled out of bed.

Dad was sitting in his favourite chair beside the front window, a cup of coffee resting on his knee as he read the paper. He peeked out from behind the sheets of print as I entered the room and went over to the tree.

'What sort of time is this to be getting up on Christmas morning?' he asked, putting aside the paper and his cup. He held out his arms, 'Merry Christmas, princess.'

I hesitated for a second. I was still mad at him for screwing up my plans to get out of the Bay but I didn't want to be the one to spoil the day, so I swallowed my resentment and accepted his hug.

'Merry Christmas, Dad,' I said, sitting on his knee as I used to do when I was a little girl. 'Is Jack up yet?'

Dad nodded, 'He's already been for a run and I think he's just gotten out of the shower. Go wish your mum a Merry Christmas and by then, he should be ready.'

'I can't believe you made him run today, Dad. It is Christmas, you know.'

'His body doesn't know it's Christmas.'

'It will once it gets a taste of Aunty Verna's Christmas cake,' I quipped, jumping up as Dad whacked me with the paper.

'There is nothing wrong with your Aunty Verna's cake,' he said sternly.

'Sure, as long as you've got an iron liver,' I teased, as I slipped down the hallway to the kitchen. 'Merry Christmas, Mum.'

She looked up at me and smiled. 'Merry Christmas to you, honey-child.' She was up to her elbows in flour so I walked behind her and gave her a hug, resting my head on her shoulder blade and enjoying the soft, fruity smell of her perfume. 'Are you ready to open your presents?' she asked, slipping from my grip. She crossed to the sink and washed her hands. Then she hurried over to the freezer and pulled out four metal trays filled with her famous watermelon sorbet.

'I'm waiting for Jack,' I said, sticking my finger into a tray and scooping some of the sweet, icy mixture into my mouth.

'Hey, get out of that,' Mum said, brandishing a wooden spoon at me. 'What's your brother doing?'

'Showering.'

Mum sighed and began to whip the sorbet. 'I remember a time when we had to practically lock the two of you in your rooms to keep you away from the presents under the tree. Now, Jack has to have a shower before he'll even look at a gift tag.' She tapped the sorbet off the spoon and carried the trays back to the freezer.

'Come on Mum, don't get all misty on me. At least you get better presents from us now.' I took her by the hand and dragged her out into the lounge room. 'Do you remember the time Jack caught that frog and wrapped it up for you as a present?'

'How could I forget? The poor little thing suffocated and stank out the whole house.'

We entered the room just as Jack appeared in the other doorway, pink-skinned from his shower. We gathered around the tree and began our usual Christmas routine. This year it was Jack's turn to hand out the presents while Mum, Dad and I patiently waited, 'ohh-ing' and 'ahh-ing' over each gift that was distributed. When all the gifts had been allocated, we began to unwrap them: Mum and Dad taking turns, enjoying the giving more than the getting, while Jack and I set upon our presents like ravenous dogs.

After the presents came breakfast - a light meal of cereal and fruit so that we didn't stuff ourselves too much before lunch - and then Mum ordered the boys out of the kitchen so that we could get everything ready while they set up the backyard with chairs, tables and glittering tinsel.

I would've preferred to help Dad in the backyard but my parents believed in equality of the sexes, which meant that one year I'd be stuck in the kitchen and the next year it would be Jack's turn. So I spent the morning running around like a blue-arsed fly, cooking, cleaning and decorating until, finally, about an hour before the first guest arrived, it was all done. I slid the last seafood platter into the fridge and stood up, a thank-God-that's-over smile on my lips, and saw Alyce leaning against the wall, staring at me.

A volley of heartbeats went off my chest. 'Holy shit, you scared the crap out of me,' I said, slamming the fridge door closed.

'Sorry, I thought you heard me come in,' she said, grinning as she looked me over. 'Why aren't you ready? Everyone will be here soon.' She glanced meaningfully through the kitchen window towards Sebastian's house.

'Don't worry. I told them to come over at 12.30 and if I've learnt anything about Sebastian's mum in the last few weeks, it's that she's always on time.' I slipped my arm through Alyce's and we walked down to my bedroom, chatting about what we got for Christmas.

Alyce threw herself across my bed and started going through my CDs while I rummaged around in my cupboard for the clothes I wanted to wear. 'You've been spending a lot of time with Sebastian's family,' she said, trying to sound casual.

I poked my head around the door and looked at her. 'Are you annoyed with me?

She shrugged. No, I was only wondering why you're over there so much, that's all.'

'I'm just being friendly, you know, getting to know my boyfriend's parents.'

'Why? Are you planning to move in with them?' She giggled, 'I bet Lilly would love that!'

'I'm not going anywhere, for now,' I said, taking

a green miniskirt from a coat hanger and a red and white striped halter neck from my drawer. I flipped them over my arm while I picked up a few other things I needed for my shower, and then I walked over to the door and turned towards Alyce. 'But if I did want to move in with the Holborns, I reckon they'd let me and there wouldn't be a damn thing Lilly could do about it.'

'So the truth finally comes out. That's the real reason you've been hanging out with Sebastian's parents, isn't it? To annoy Lilly.'

I chuckled. 'No, that's a bonus.'

'Well, what do you do over there?'

'Nothing really. Just hang out with Sebastian or help Clare around the house.'

Alyce raised an eyebrow. 'Jack told me that you took them up to the lighthouse. What was that about?'

'I don't know. Sebastian's dad is into all that maritime history crap, so I took them up there for a picnic. I also took them to Deception Beach to look at the wreck of The Emu. Is that a crime?'

'No,' Alyce said, glancing at me from the corner of her eye.

'What's that look for?' I asked, impatiently.

'Sometimes I don't understand you, Mira.'

'What's to understand? They're Sebastian's parents and I'm getting to know them.'

Alyce rolled onto her stomach and picked up a different CD and, as I headed off for my shower, I heard her mutter, 'Yeah right, if only it was that simple.'

A little later, as Alyce finished winding some green ribbon through my hair, we heard the doorbell. I looked at my watch and saw that it was 12.30 p.m.

'What did I tell you?' I said, as we scurried out of my room and down the hallway. I quickly straightened my skirt and smoothed down my hair - Alyce rolled her eyes and slapped my hand away - and then I pulled open the door.

Clare and William stood before us, their arms filled with Christmas stuff. My eyes were immediately drawn to the large silver tray with a massive golden-brown turkey trussed upon it that William carried.

'One turkey as promised,' Clare said, smiling broadly at me and I couldn't help but smile back.

'It looks delicious,' I said, stepping aside to let them into the house.

Sebastian was standing behind them, looking hot in a red Mongoose T-shirt and long black shorts, and next to him was Lilly. She looked stunning in a long daffodil yellow dress and matching shoes. The only thing brighter than her outfit was her smile. I frowned a little. *Why is she so happy*? I wondered.

'Merry Christmas, Mira. Merry Christmas, Alyce,' Lilly said, cheerfully as she stepped into my house. 'Which way is it to the party?' She wandered off towards the backyard, following the voices and Christmas carols.

Alyce glanced at me and I could read my own confusion in her eyes. *What the hell was Lilly playing at*? It took us a second to recover from our shock and then we spluttered out our own Christmas greetings to her retreating back.

William held the turkey in one hand and patted my shoulder. 'It seems the goodwill fairy finally caught up with our Lilly last night. Enjoy it while it lasts,' he said, as he strolled after his daughter.

'Oh, William, she's not that bad,' Clare scolded,

as she handed me two bottles of wine and followed her husband through the house.

I didn't like the sound of that.

I passed the bottles to Alyce and asked her to put them in the kitchen for me as I took Sebastian's hand. I reached up and kissed him quickly on the lips. He tried to catch me in his arms but I pushed him gently away. 'Later,' I promised, leading him out into the backyard.

Lilly and her parents were already at the table that Dad and Jack had set up under the lilac-covered jacaranda that dominated our yard. Mum had cleared a space for the turkey and was busy hugging Clare and William, who both looked slightly uncomfortable in her embrace.

Our other guests, the Wilsons and their three brats from next door and my parents' oldest friends, Art and Bettina Hancock, were chatting noisily among themselves. At the head of the table, closest to the toilet, was my Aunty Verna who was deep in conversation with Mr Harris from the pharmacy. He seemed to be listening carefully and I shook my head. *What did old people have to talk about?* I wondered. *How close they were to dying.*

I smiled and called 'Merry Christmas' to all of them but I didn't stop to talk. I was more interested in saving Clare from Mum's stranglehold. I slipped in between them and Clare gave me a grateful look as she turned her attention to my dad. He was standing beside Michael and Danny Parish on the opposite side of table, his hand resting proudly on Jack's shoulder, as he bleated on and on about Jack's latest sporting achievements.

After about five minutes of polite nodding, I noticed a look pass between the Holborns. I sighed and looked into the distance as if I was trying to ignore the pain caused by my father's constant praise of Jack. Clare inched over to me and softly rubbed my arm to let me know I wasn't forgotten.

'Okay, that's enough talk about sport,' Mum said, tapping a spoon against a glass. She waited while we took our seats and then she continued, 'It's time to celebrate Christmas with our friends, both old and new.'

'Here! Here!' Dad said, raising his glass.

I looked over at Sebastian and grimaced, but he just smiled and took a swallow of his drink. My eyes wandered as everyone chatted back and forth across the table. Finally, they came to rest on Lilly. She was sitting at the end of the table, between Alyce and my Aunty Verna, and she didn't look so happy any more.

The afternoon progressed as it had since I was a small child. There was a lot of eating and much drinking by the adults, while us kids - except for Lilly - jumped in the pool or played video games until we got bored. Later in the day, we took a stroll down to the break-wall and watched the dolphins playing in the current for a while, until we grew bored with that too. On the way back, Sebastian and I ducked into the bushes and spent a breathless few moments exploring each other's mouths and bodies until Jack, Alyce and Danny found us and started making loud retching noises, drawing the attention of the passing tourists who infested the Bay at that time of year.

When we got back to our house, I found my parents chatting comfortably with the Holborns. They laughed suddenly and clinked their wine glasses together. Somehow, I knew they were talking about me.

'What do you make of that?' I asked Sebastian as we slid into the pool for another swim.

He gave the adults an uninterested look, then wrapped his arm around my belly and dragged me into deeper water. 'Nothing. They're just talking, and as long as they're doing that they're not watching us.' He kissed my neck and his hand stroked the curve of my breast.

I shivered and pulled out of his grasp. 'They're not watching but other people are,' I said, nodding to the far end of the pool where Lilly was glaring at us with flat, spite-filled eyes. She turned away and stomped across the grass to the table where she flung herself into a chair next to my Aunty Verna.

'Well, there goes the Christmas cheer,' Sebastian muttered as we swam back to the edge.

'She'll get over it,' I said, watching Lilly closely.

My Aunty Verna tapped her on the shoulder and Lilly turned to talk to her, but not before I noticed the sly look on her face. *What are you telling my sweet old aunty*? I wondered, as I climbed out of the pool. I dried off and wrapped the towel around my waist, keeping my eyes fixed on Lilly. 'I'll be back in a minute,' I said, leaving Sebastian in the pool.

As I approached them, my Aunty Verna abruptly stood up and shuffled off in the direction of the house. I watched her cross the lawn then I went over to Lilly, who was leaning back in her chair looking like someone who had just gobbled the last chocolate.

'What did you say to my aunty?' I demanded.

At first, she pretended not to hear, but I wasn't going to play that game. I folded my arms and waited for her to respond. When she saw that I wasn't going to repeat myself, she raised a hand to shade her eyes. 'What did I say to whom?' she asked, sweetly.

'God, you're such a child. No wonder your parents think you're a nutcase.'

Lilly sprang out of the chair and slammed her hands into my chest, sending me flying backwards. I waved my arms and tried to stay on my feet but I tripped over Mrs Wilson's handbag and landed with a heavy thud on my butt. The Wilson children - the little creeps - laughed and Lilly smirked, but only for a moment.

'Lilly Holborn! What do you think you are doing?' Clare's voice cut across the afternoon. Her face was a thundercloud of anger as she stalked over to us. 'How dare you treat Mira like that and embarrass us in front of our hosts!'

A huddle of concerned adults crowded around me as Alyce and her dad helped me to my feet. I got up slowly, hissing as spears of pain shot through my back. The tears in my eyes were real and as they rolled down my cheeks, Clare lost the plot completely.

'Goddamn it, you horrid child, you've spoiled your last Christmas,' she said.

'No, wait. Mrs Holborn,' I said, as Michael eased me into a chair. 'I'm okay. I just tripped, that's all.'

Sebastian, dripping from the pool, took my hand and glared at his sister. 'Don't stick up for her, Mira. I saw her push you. What were you thinking, Lilly?'

Lilly returned his angry stare defiantly but I could see the shimmer of tears in her eyes and I almost felt sorry for her.

Until Mum butted in. 'Now, just hold on a

second,' she said, using her placating voice. 'I know my daughter and she may not be as innocent as she appears. What part did you play in this, Mira?'

'Really, Susan. We all saw what happened,' William said. He sounded almost offended by my mum's question. 'It doesn't matter what Mira did, if she did anything at all, there is never any excuse for an act of violence.'

Mum, however, wasn't having any of that and neither was my dad. He knelt down beside the chair and looked at me. 'What did you say to provoke Lilly? I want the truth,' he said.

I sniffed loudly and looked up as Danny slipped some tissues into my hand. 'Thank you, Dan,' I said, wiping my eyes and gently blowing my nose. 'I didn't do anything to her, Dad...'

'You're a bloody liar,' Lilly snapped.

Her father sent her a look that would have quenched the fires of hell and Lilly immediately shut her mouth.

I swallowed and then went on, 'She was talking to Aunty Verna...'

'Did someone say my name? Why is everyone crowded around Mira? Is she telling a story? Oh, I love a good story. Mind you, it's my Jackie-boy who tells the best stories. Do you remember the one about the lady and the tiger? Oh, that was my favourite,' she cackled and clapped her hands in delight.

Jack had been standing beside Sebastian. With a small signal from Mum, he stepped over to Aunty Verna. 'Would you like me to tell you that story now, Aunty?' he asked, guiding her towards the house.

When they were out of earshot, I began again. 'Lilly was sitting by herself and I thought she might like someone - other than Aunty Verna - to talk to. She looked kind of lonely so I came over, but when I asked her what she was doing, she called me a slut for kissing Sebastian. Then she shoved me away from her and I fell over.' I tried to sit a little straighter in the chair and winced as the pain shot through my back.

'We might have to get her to the doctor,' Michael Parish said, squeezing my hand, 'just to make sure there is no spinal damage.' He smiled at me reassuringly. 'There won't be but it's always best to be sure.'

'I think I'll be fine if I walk around for a bit, Mr Parish,' I said.

'Oh, pleeaasse,' Lilly muttered.

'That's enough from you,' Clare said.

'What? You're falling for this? It's bullshit. I didn't call her a slut and her back is just fine. She didn't even fall that hard.'

'I've heard enough,' William said, in a tone that allowed no argument. 'Go home, Lilly. Your cold and callous behaviour is not welcome here.'

Lilly stared at him for a moment and then looked into her mother's hostile eyes. Her mouth thinned to an angry red slash and I waited for an outburst, but she just lifted her chin and walked out of our backyard without looking back.

Clare and William left soon after, with a promise that Lilly would be punished severely for her actions. My mum and dad tried to convince them that it wasn't all that serious - never mind that I was having trouble walking - and to be lenient with Lilly.

'After all,' Mum said, as she walked them to the front door, 'Jack and Mira have these sort of teenage brawls all the time. And I can assure you that most of the time, it's Mira who instigates them. Perhaps you should give Lilly the benefit of the doubt this time.'

'Gee, thanks Mum,' I said, as I shuffled past them on my way to the car.

William hurried down the steps and opened the door for me. 'I'm sorry Lilly ruined your Christmas Day, Mira. And I hope everything is okay at the doctor's,' he said.

'Thanks, but I'll be fine. I'm just happy that we got to spend most of the day together.'

He smiled at me and said, 'Well if you need anything, just let me know.'

'There is one thing,' I said, before he closed the door. He raised an inquiring eyebrow. 'Would Sebastian be able to come with me?'

'If he wants to,' he replied, and before he finished the sentence, Sebastian was sitting on the seat beside me. 'Well, I guess he does.' He slammed the door shut and tapped the roof, as though Michael Parish was a driver for the Secret Service and I was royalty.

My spine was okay, although I did have a bruised tailbone, and that was pretty uncomfortable for a week or so. But I happily accepted the pain when I heard that the Holborns had sent Lilly to stay with her cousin in Brisbane for a couple of weeks. I'd fought the war and won. Lilly was out of the way and I had Sebastian and his family all to myself.

Nothing could stop me from getting out of the Bay now.

ITEM THREE

Email #3.

Retrieved from hard drive belonging to: Mira Falling (Age 18)

Point of Origin and Authorship Indeterminable

<u>From</u>: <bonnie@barrowgang.com>

<u>To</u>: <fallingstar@email.com.au>

<u>Sent</u>: Saturday, 7 January 2013 5:45AM

<u>Subject</u>: Fw: Stand By Your Man

Mira,

You've read the story of Bonnie and Clyde,
Of how they lived and how they died,
Love's devotion their one true emotion,
That even death could not cast aside.

Now read the story of Mira and 'Bastian,
Young lovers' destiny will guide,
His heart, faithfully hold, his coveted soul,
And never let the bonds that bind divide.

Bonnie Parker

Assessment: As with the N.K. and Saucy Jack emails, the source of the Bonnie Parker email has yet to be determined. A preliminary search of account holders in the name of Bonnie Parker has failed to establish a connection to Mira Falling.

TEN

You know, as little brothers go, Jack wasn't so bad. Sure, I could have strangled him sometimes - like when he started charging his friends entry to my room so they could check out my underwear - but, mostly, he was good to have around. We didn't argue too much and, until Sebastian moved into the Bay, we were going places together.

But then, a couple of weekends before my eighteenth birthday, everything changed.

I woke up in a crappy mood on the Saturday morning of that fateful weekend, mainly because I had to open the pharmacy by myself while Dad went into Bridgewater to buy *more* running gear for Jack. Talk about favouritism.

He never bought anything for me but if Jack so much as hinted that his little toe *might* be feeling cramped inside his runners, Dad would be on the phone ordering a new pair of shoes and anything else he thought Jack might need. And what did I get? The opportunity to work my arse off in our stupid bloody shop. Lucky me.

Don't get me wrong. I didn't care that Jack got stuff. I knew how things were with him. He was

Dad's golden boy, his ticket to fame and glory, but it really got up my nose that I had to sacrifice my time just so the little freak-boy could have his every whim taken care of.

I confronted my dad about this injustice on Friday afternoon while he was reading the newspaper on the veranda. 'Why do you have to go into Bridgewater tomorrow? Jack's got enough running gear. Hell, he could probably loan some to the whole Australian sprint team.'

Dad looked at me over the top of his reading glasses and sighed as he folded the paper into his lap. 'First of all, Mira, you will not use that language in my house. Secondly, we've given you a job at the pharmacy so you can buy your own things. Your brother can't work because of his training schedule, so he relies on us to get him what he needs,' he explained in the annoyingly patient voice that he used with our crabbier customers.

I gritted my teeth, determined not to lose my temper. 'I don't care if you buy Jack his own sports store. Why can't he work at the pharmacy tomorrow? He doesn't have training. You gave him the day off, remember?'

'Jack needs time to relax too, Mira. Surely, you don't begrudge him that? Besides, I'm sure you'll find a way to spend the extra money. Wasn't there a dress or something you wanted to buy?' He shook the paper out, ruffling the pages dismissively, and was soon lost in the day's headlines.

End of discussion.

I threw off my tangled sheets and sat on the edge of my bed. Our house was quiet. Dad had already left for Bridgewater, and Mum and Jack were still asleep.

At least I'd have the place to myself for a while.

Before I headed to the bathroom for a shower, I grabbed my phone. I needed to message Alyce and Sebastian about the change in my plans for the day.

That was the other reason I was so pissed off.

Sebastian's dad was taking him into Bridgewater to pick up his new car - an eighteenth birthday present - and he'd asked Alyce and me to go along. We hardly ever got to go 'into town' (as my mother called it) by ourselves and we were looking forward to doing some serious shopping without our mothers nagging us.

Until my dad stuffed up my plans.

When I got back from my shower, I could see the email icon flashing on my phone. I guessed it'd be from Alyce - she always wanted advice on what to wear, though why she was emailing me was a mystery - so I threw on some clothes and opened the email.

But it wasn't from Alyce. It was from some chick called Bonnie Parker, and attached to it was a poem about Sebastian and me.

Now I was seriously pissed off. Not only did I have to work and miss out on a day of shopping with my friends, but I also had to put up with more of Jack's idiotic email pranks. I was sick of it.

I stomped down to his room, grabbed one of his pillows, and whacked him across the head. 'What the hell?' he mumbled, sitting up in his bed and blinking.

'Listen, you little shit. Stop sending me those stupid emails. Whatever is going on between Sebastian and me is my business. Got it!' I said, shoving my finger into his chest.

He pushed my hand away and sprang up like a

Jack-in-the-box. 'What's your bloody problem?'

'You are,' I said. 'So quit your games and stay out of my life.' I spun away and walked out of the room.

'I don't know what you're talking about,' Jack said, following me into the hallway. 'I haven't sent you any emails.'

'Sure. Just like you didn't send me that email when Mrs Johnson died, right? God, isn't it time you grew up?' I said, turning to face him.

Jack's hands clenched into fists and he glared at me. 'I told you, Mira. I didn't send you any emails. Not then. Not now. And I don't give a damn about you and Sebastian. Although I can't figure out what he sees in a feral, no-talent cow like you.'

A thin red veil slipped over my eyes and my hands curled into claws, as the words 'no talent' rolled around inside my head. 'You little bastard,' I yelled, as I flew at him, raking my nails across his face.

He grabbed my arms and slammed me into the wall, making Mum's favourite Salvador Dali print bounce and clatter to the floor. I screamed and kicked out, getting him in the thigh (although I was aiming higher) and he yelped with pain. I seized a handful of his hair and dragged him towards the floor, wanting to pound those ugly words out of his mouth, but as I pulled his head back, I felt his fist sink deep into my stomach.

Suddenly I was lying on the floor, breathing in carpet dust as I tried to cough and swallow at the same time. I felt vomit at the back of my throat and I tried to force it away. *Is this what it feels like to die*? I wondered, and a picture of Mrs Johnson, her mouth stuffed with chocolate muffins, flashed into my head.

From far away, I heard Mum's voice, raised in sleepy confusion. 'What is going on out there?'

Jack muttered something and then I felt Mum's arms lock around my chest as she dragged me to my feet. New waves of pain burst across my stomach and drilled into my back as she led me to my room and helped me down onto my bed.

The air seeped back into my lungs and the pain eased to a throbbing ache at the centre of my body. I looked into Mum's face, feeling like a five-year-old again, but there was no sympathy in her eyes.

'What was that about, Mira?' she demanded as she sat down. 'I wake up to find you two going at each other like a couple of street fighters. You know we don't treat each other like that in this family. For goodness sake, just look at your brother's face.'

Jack stared down at me, his cheek slashed with four raised welts. 'He deserved it,' I wheezed.

'Really?' Mum said, raising her eyebrows. 'Well, in that case, you'll deserve the punishment I decide on.'

Jack smirked as she got up off my bed and stood next to him. 'You'd better hurry up and get ready. Your father expects the shop to be open by nine,' she said, pushing Jack towards the hallway. As they went through the door, I heard her going off at Jack, but I knew she wouldn't punish him. That was the advantage of having *potential*.

I stayed on my bed for a long time, watching my clock click towards eight, waiting for the pain in my stomach to fade. When it was just a dull ache, I crawled over to my computer and had a closer look at the mysterious poem that had caused the whole thing.

I was pretty sure that I didn't know anyone called Bonnie Parker, although there was a Gina Parker in the year below me at school, but I'd never spoken to her. There was something about the name that was familiar, though. It buzzed in my brain as I stared at the email. Maybe I was thinking of one of the summer girls who came up to the Bay with their families every year. I knew most of them, but I couldn't remember anyone called Bonnie.

I read through the verse again, staring at the names - Bonnie and Clyde - why were they so familiar? Were they friends of my parents? Or a distant aunt and uncle? Maybe they were an old movie star couple that I'd seen on the TV.

Mum would know, but I didn't think she'd be in the mood to talk to me. Dad might know but he was out of town and as for Jack, there was no way in hell I was going to ask that little scumbag anything. So, I turned to the only place where I knew I'd be able to get some answers - the Internet.

I fired up my search engine and typed in the name 'Bonnie Parker' and, in a few seconds, had 14,500,000 hits. As soon as I read the first listing, I knew why the names were familiar. I had seen them on the TV, but they weren't movie stars.

About six months ago, Mum and Dad made us sit through a documentary on infamous criminals. (I hate it when they hog the TV.) Bonnie and Clyde, I remembered, were lovers who had gone on a bank-robbing and killing spree across America in the 1930s. And, as the picture in front of me showed, they had died in a hail of bullets when the police had ambushed their car on a quiet country road.

The question was why had someone sent me an

email pretending to be a dead outlaw? And why write a poem about Sebastian and me? I could see what it was trying to tell me - Sebastian and I were meant to be together and I shouldn't let anything come between us - but who was behind it?

My fingers absently beat out a rhythm on the desktop as I thought about the people I knew. There was no way it was from someone at school. I hadn't given my email address to any of those losers and, besides, no one at school even knew about Sebastian. I sat up a little straighter in my chair. 'Did he send it to me?' I asked wondered aloud.

I swivelled around in my chair and stared through my window. Sending me a poem was kind of romantic (in a dorky sort of way) but was *Love's devotion their one true emotion* something Sebastian would write? Wasn't he more of a *Roses are red, Violets are blue, I want to get into your pants and under your bra too* kind of guy? And why sign the poem with a girl's name? No, the more I thought about it, the more convinced I was that Sebastian hadn't sent the email.

Maybe it was Lilly. Ha! That was a laugh. She fucking hated me. I tried to imagine Lilly composing a love poem about Sebastian and me but I couldn't do it. Instead, an image of her sticking pins in a doll - which bore a freakish resemblance to me - while she passed it back and forth over a candle and chanted 'Die! Die! Die!' flashed into my head. I grinned and mentally crossed her off the list.

As for Alyce and Danny, I didn't even bother to consider them. Alyce was my best friend and if she had something to say about Sebastian, she would've told to my face. And Danny? Well, only three things mattered to him - cars, computer games and football. If anyone even mentioned the word 'love', he'd start dry retching.

That left Jack.

I hit the reply icon and quickly typed up a note, telling Jack that I was sorry and wanted to make peace. I knew he wouldn't reply - he might have been a loser but he wasn't stupid - so I planned to sneak into his room later and check his email. If my note was on his computer, that would prove he was 'Bonnie Parker'. Then I'd have it out with him again, and this time Mum would have to be on my side.

I clicked the 'send' button and the email zipped into cyberspace. I rubbed the tender place on my belly and smiled. *Let's see you get out of this, Jack*, I thought, but as I shifted the mouse to exit the program, an email arrived in my mailbox. I frowned. It was the same message from Bonnie Parker.

I bolted for Jack's room, expecting to see him at his computer, but the room was empty and his computer screen was a black lifeless square. At the far end of the hallway, the shower hissed and a wisp of steam slipped from beneath the bathroom door. I walked slowly back to my room and stood in front of my computer, staring at the message on the screen. Who had sent it and why? Was it the same person who had sent the Ned Kelly and Jack the Ripper emails? If so, what were they trying to tell me?

Ned Kelly. Jack the Ripper. Bonnie Parker. What did they have in common, other than being infamous murderers?

Suddenly, a blast of music filled the room. I gave a little shout of surprise and dived across my bed, pounding on my alarm clock to shut it off. It was twenty to nine. I couldn't worry about the emails any more. I had to get to the pharmacy. The last thing I needed was my old man spewing at me for not opening on time.

I shut down my computer. The mystery of Bonnie Parker would have to wait until later. I quickly got my stuff together and then climbed out the window - I didn't want to see Mum or my weasel brother - and ran all the way to Main Street.

ELEVEN

Mr Harris was sitting on a milk crate beside the back entrance to our shop when I bolted around the corner. He was a semi-retired pharmacist who sometimes filled in for Dad on weekends. I really liked him, although he was pretty old. He loved to freak me out with his gory war stories - like the one about the American GIs who beheaded a Vietnamese soldier and hung his head in a tree for his mates to find - and he'd always stick up for me when Dad was getting on my case.

'Morning, Mira,' he said, getting to his feet.

'Hi, Mr Harris, have you been waiting long?' I asked, as I fumbled with the keys to the back door.

'No, just got here myself.' He took the keys from me and slid them into the lock. 'Relax, kid. You ain't late, yet. And even if you were, it'd be our little secret.'

I smiled at him. 'Thanks, Mr Harris, but Mrs Gordon is waiting out the front.'

'Oh, cripes! Quick, get the lights on and the front door open, or that old busy-body will have us both in trouble,' he said, shooing me inside.

As I walked through the shop, turning on the lights as I went, the front door rattled against its frame. I checked my watch and saw that it was just past the hour. I sighed and plastered on a smile.

Mrs Gordon stood under the eaves; one liver-spotted hand wrapped around the knob of her walking stick, the other planted on her bony hip.

'Good morning, Mrs Gordon,' I said.

She sniffed and looked down at her watch. 'It's about time, Mira Falling. Your father always opens before nine,' she said, hobbling into the shop.

'Sorry.'

'You should be. Young people today have no respect for the elderly.'

Here we go, I thought.

Mrs Gordon was the first in a long line of whiney old farts who felt it was their God-given right to lecture me on what was wrong with everyone under the age of twenty-one. By lunchtime, I was so fed up with listening to them that I felt like shoving their prescriptions down their scrawny throats.

The lowest point of my day, however, came when the Batemans decided to have a totally disgusting debate over haemorrhoid creams. They kept asking my opinion, as though I'm some great expert on anal problems. God, just thinking about it made me want to hurl.

I turned away from them, pretending to look for something on the shelf, and saw Lilly step through the door. My heart skipped a beat and then sped up a little one of as it usually did when she was around. It was those fight or flight kind of things; except I wouldn't have run away from her even if she'd been carrying a bazooka, so maybe it was more of a fight or *fight* kind of thing. Whatever it was, I was ready for her.

She'd been back in town for about a week, but

this was the first time I'd seen her. Even when I dropped into Sebastian's place, which was almost every day, she stayed in her room. I figured that she was sulking over her weeks in exile but, watching the way she looked around the shop with her usual condescending confidence, I began to think that I should reconsider my ideas.

She didn't come directly to the counter, but slipped into the cosmetics aisle where she started testing the perfumes and lipsticks as if she were shopping in a big city department store. Occasionally she would look over the shelves and glare at me. I tried to ignore her and focus on what the Batemans were saying, but having Lilly in the shop was like having a splinter rammed under my thumbnail. I had to get her out.

'Excuse me for a minute,' I said, and Mrs Bateman waved a flabby arm at me and went on jabbing a tube of cream into her husband's chest.

Mr Harris was in the dispensary, mixing up the powders and potions that kept our older customers alive day after day. I knocked on the door. 'Excuse me, Mr Harris, could you come and help the Batemans before they start wrestling over the haemorrhoid creams?'

Mr Harris chuckled. 'Ah, the joy of getting old,' he said, putting an arm around my shoulder. 'See what you have to look forward to, young lady.'

'Great,' I replied.

As soon as Mrs Bateman saw Mr Harris, she grabbed him by the arm and dragged him into the argument. He glanced at me and shrugged helplessly as different creams were shoved into his hand. I grinned and then went in search of Lilly.

I found her at the front of the shop. She was leaning against a shelf, watching a pod of dolphins frolicking beside the break-wall across the road. Her lips were curled into a soft smile and, as always, I was surprise by the similarity between her and Sebastian. Then, she turned towards me, her smile disappearing as she looked me up and down, and I remembered that, although they looked similar, they were very different people. Sebastian was warm and loving, but Lilly was an ice queen, and that made her easy to hate.

'What do you want?' I said.

'I want you to leave Jack alone,' she replied, bluntly.

'Jack who?' I asked, thinking she must be talking about one of the summer kids.

'You really are dumb,' she sneered, staring at me like I was fungus. 'Your *brother*. I saw what you did to him and I'm telling you to leave him alone.'

I stared at her, amazed at her nerve. It was as though she hadn't been away at all. 'As if trying to break me and Sebastian up wasn't bad enough, now *you're* telling me to stay away from my own brother. Man, what planet are you living on?'

She didn't get a chance to answer. Mrs Bateman came bustling through the store carrying a small blue paper bag and, from the satisfied smirk on her face, it looked like she had won the debate.

Lilly slipped away as Mrs Bateman wobbled up to me and said, 'Thank you for your help, Mira. We'll have Harold sitting down without that awful whoopee cushion in no time.'

'That's great, Mrs Bateman,' I said, as her husband - his ears flaming red - grabbed her arm and pulled her into the street.

As the door clicked shut behind them, Lilly reappeared.

'Is that what you imagine for you and Sebastian?' she asked, watching the Batemans shuffling, arm in arm, down the street. She tilted her head and laughed softly. 'It's never going to happen, you know. You're just a temporary *plaything* for my brother. You amuse him now, but next month there'll be someone new.'

'I don't think so. Sebastian and I are meant for each other.'

'Really? Does he know that?' Lilly asked, arching her perfect eyebrows.

'Yeah, he does,' I said, stepping closer. I ran my fingernail along the line of her jaw. She pulled her head away and glared at me.

'Don't touch me,' she said.

'Why not? From what I've seen you like being touched by your relatives, and since we're almost sisters…' I trailed off, leaving her to fill in the blanks.

'Keep dreaming, bitch.'

I looked at her closely and smiled. 'You're just pissed off because Sebastian's found something better than sisterly love,' I taunted.

Her face darkened with anger. 'You'll never replace me,' she said.

'I already have,' I replied.

She looked ready to tear my face off, and I think she would have tried, but the front door suddenly banged open and Danny came barrelling into the shop, followed closely by his sister.

'What's going on here?' Alyce asked.

'Nothing,' Lilly said, stepping away.

'We were just talking about Jack and Sebastian,' I said.

'Really? You and Lilly were talking?' A puzzled look clouded Alyce's face.

I was about to answer her when Danny tugged on my arm. 'Mira! Guess what sort of car Sebastian got for his birthday?' he said.

Alyce groaned and grabbed my other arm. 'Hey, is that Mr Harris down there?' she asked, trying to drag me away from her brother. 'I haven't talked to him for ages. Come on, Mira. You can... umm... introduce me — again.'

I pulled away and looked at Danny. 'I don't know anything about cars, Dan. So, why don't you just tell me what Sebastian got, okay?'

'Don't say I didn't warn you,' Alyce murmured, as she wandered over to Mr Harris.

Danny looked at me blankly for a moment, his hair falling over his green eyes. Then he made the connection. 'Oh, yeah, it's a twin-cam turbo Supra, with fat mags and extractors and the coolest paint job,' he said, excitedly. 'Just wait 'til you see it, Mira. It's so low you can almost feel the road scraping under your feet.'

That was the funny thing about Danny. He could be as thick as two bricks about most things but he knew cars like a priest knows his bible. It came naturally to him - like Alyce with her flute - and he'd been tinkering around with his dad's cars ever since he was old enough to lift the bonnet.

''Wow! That's so cool,' I said.

'Yeah, but the best thing is, he's going to let me drive it.'

'In your dreams, moron. Sebastian would never

let anyone drive his car,' Lilly said, slinking back into the aisle.

'Yeah, he would. He's letting me. We're gonna take a run along Prospect Road tomorrow,' Danny said.

'Listen up, dull-boy. If anyone's driving that car, it's me,' Lilly said, looking Danny up and down in that rich bitch way that made me want to punch her face in. 'How old are you, anyway? Not old enough for a licence, that's for sure.'

'Don't need a licence,' Danny muttered, staring down at the floor.

'*Hello*? If you're gonna drive my brother's car, you do,' Lilly said, and then she laughed. 'What the hell am I talking about? There's no way Sebastian would let an unlicensed, uninsured retard like you drive his car.'

'Knock off the retard crap, Lilly. Danny's been driving since he was ten,' I said, putting my arm around him. 'And he could take you any day of the week.'

'Really?'

'Yeah. Really.'

She stood, looking from me to Danny and back again, and I could almost read her thoughts as she weighed the possibilities. 'So, what are you suggesting? A race between Mr Potato-Head and me?'

I hadn't actually been thinking of a race, but now that Lilly had brought it up, it made bizarre kind of sense. I glanced towards the back of the shop, making sure Alyce was still busy talking to Mr Harris. She'd never agree to Danny racing, although it was the way kids in the Bay sometimes settled things. Even my dad had raced along Prospect Road when he was a kid - racing was how he got his first car (and if my Uncle Phil was right, how he got his first girl-friend too).

'That's right. A race between you and Danny. Along the Prospect Road. Tomorrow afternoon. What do you say?'

'Can I race Sebastian's car?' Danny asked, excited again.

'No,' Lilly snapped.

'Then what will I drive?'

I squeezed his hand, reassuringly. 'Don't worry, Dan, we'll work something out.'

'If we're going to race, let's make it worthwhile,' Lilly said. She had a sly look on her face.

'Worthwhile? How?' I inquired.

'Well, what about this,' she said slowly, as if the idea had just occurred to her. 'If Dumbo here wins, you get Sebastian and I won't try to break you up any more. But if I win, you find yourself a new boyfriend and leave me and *my* brother alone.'

'You'd give up your brother just like that? I thought twins were inseparable?'

'We are inseparable. And no matter what happens, you'll never love him the way I do. Now do you want to take the bet or not?'

I turned away and looked out the window, thinking hard. What if Danny lost the race? Could I give up Sebastian that easily?

As if he had read my thoughts, Danny said, 'Don't worry, Mira. I can take her.'

I smiled at the determination in his voice. It was the most beautiful thing about Danny. It didn't matter what he was asked to do, he always believed that he could do it.

'Who can you take and where?' Alyce asked, coming up behind us.

'I can take her. In a race,' Danny crowed.

Lilly snorted. 'Yeah, right. Lucky you don't need brains to drive, Dopey, or the race would be over before you even hit the accelerator.'

'Hey! Don't talk to my brother like that,' Alyce said. She gripped my arm and swung me around to face them. 'What are they talking about, Mira?'

'Not now, Alyce,' I said, locking my eyes onto Lilly's. 'Okay, you're on. But, if you don't turn up, he's mine.'

'Who's yours?' Alyce demanded.

'Fine,' Lilly replied, ignoring her. She opened the door and held it with her foot while she slipped on her sunnies. 'Later, losers,' she said.

'Would someone *please* tell me what the hell is going on?'

'Me and Lilly are having a race,' Danny said, putting his arm around Alyce. 'And I'm going to kick her butt so Mira can keep being Sebastian's girlfriend.' Colour flared in his cheeks and he grinned as though he'd said something naughty.

'That's the best idea I've heard all day, Danny,' I said, ruffling his hair.

'Mira?'

I turned to Alyce and saw the gentle curve of her mouth harden as understanding filled her eyes and I quickly looped my arm through hers, leading her deeper into the shop before she could launch into a sermon about responsibility. I needed to convince her to let Danny race and that wasn't going to be easy, but I knew that I would talk her around eventually.

TWELVE

When I was a kid, my dad proclaimed Sunday as Family Day. We'd go to Church in the morning and then spend the rest of the day together, fishing or bushwalking or, sometimes, catching a movie in Bridgewater. It was great - when I was ten - but my dad refused to move with the times and, by the time Jack was fifteen, we were totally over Family Day.

There was no getting out of it, though, and even sickness (unless contagious) couldn't save us from the boredom and embarrassment of hanging out with our parents. The only reprieve came on the last Sunday afternoon of the month when Mum and Dad played bridge with their friends, Art and Bettina Hancock.

Everything about Art Hancock screamed heart attack, from his nicotine-stained fingers to the rolls of flesh that hung around his middle, like pizza dough. Despite his large size, he had small, ferrety eyes that were always trying to look down my top or up my skirt when he thought no one was watching. Bettina was also an 'ample' woman - not fat as she persistently reminded us - with a foghorn laugh and the biggest boobs I'd ever seen. She was warm and funny and I liked her a lot, although I tried to avoid her when she was with her creepy husband.

On the Sunday afternoon of the race, however, I was more than happy to see them both. They would keep my parents busy while Danny, Alyce and I took care of our business with Lilly. I opened the front door and showed them through to the back veranda where Mum and Dad were waiting. As I walked, I could feel Art's eyes crawling over my back, legs and butt, and I wished that I was wearing a shapeless sack instead of a white halter neck and red shorts.

'Is it okay if I go now, Mum?' I asked when everyone had finished hugging or shaking hands and they were seated around the table.

'Sure, love. Is Jack going with you?' she replied, as she shuffled her favourite deck of cards.

Art was staring at my breasts, his eyes moist. He licked his pudgy lips and I shuddered. 'No, he's doing something else,' I said, wrapping my arms over my chest. I glared at Art, who blinked and quickly looked down at his cards. *That's right, look away, you sick bastard,* I thought, stepping backwards through the door. I wasn't going to give him another opportunity to perv on my bum.

I raced through the house, grabbing my bag as I passed the lounge, and ducked out the front door, letting the screen door crash behind me. Mum yelled something indistinct from the back veranda but I ignored her and headed across the road.

Alyce and Danny lived on the opposite corner in a small house that their father was slowly renovating. From the front, the house looked beautiful but around the back was a junkyard of paint tins, discarded wood, old floor tiles and other bits of rubbish. I picked my way through and went over to the garage. I could hear Alyce and Danny inside, arguing over something. I smiled and bashed on the door.

'What are you kids doing in there?' I demanded, in my deepest voice.

There was the sound of scrabbling inside and then the door swung open. Jack stood in the gap, looking at me steadily, his mouth a slash of disapproval.

'What are you doing here?' I said shoving past him into the gloomy garage.

'I heard about the race,' he said. He grasped my wrist and yanked me around to face him, ready to say more but Danny's muffled voice interrupted him

'Jack's going to be my pit-crew. Isn't that cool, Mira?' he called from somewhere inside the car.

'Great,' I replied, pulling free of my brother and looking around for Alyce. She was sitting on a fold-out chair in the corner, chewing nervously on her thumb. I opened another chair and sat down beside her. 'Hey, what're you doing?'

'Nothing.'

'I can see that.' I drummed my fingers on my knees, waiting for her to say something else, but she kept her lips pressed together as tightly as a zip-locked bag. 'So, where is your dad?' I asked, drawing the question out as though I was speaking to someone simple.

Alyce gave me a withering look. 'At the pizzeria, getting a new oven installed.'

'What the hell is wrong with you?' I asked, a little too sharply. 'You look like you're about to wet your pants or something.'

She stood up suddenly, overturning the chair.

'What's wrong with me? Oh, nothing except that we're about to boost my dad's car so that my brother - who, in case you forgot, doesn't have a licence - can drive it in a stupid race that you organised, just so you can get one up on Lilly Holborn.' She grabbed the chair and set it on its feet, then sat again and folded her arms.

God, she was such a drama queen.

'Look, we're not boosting the car, we're just borrowing it. We'll have it back in plenty of time and your dad will never even know it was gone,' I reassured her.

'And what about the race?'

I shook my head impatiently. 'It'll be fine. Danny's a good driver, Alyce. Have a bit of faith in him.' I left her to think about it and walked over to the boys, trailing my fingers along the body of the car as I went.

Danny was behind the steering wheel, lovingly rubbing his hand over its smooth curve. He brushed a fleck of dirt from the dashboard and a sweet, happy grin lit up his face. He'd been working on the Lancer all summer, tinkering with its engine and attaching scrounged body parts from the wrecking yard in Bridgewater, as he slowly turned it from a kitten to a beast.

Although his father owned the car, it *belonged* to Danny. He could tell you everything about it, down to the sound of the lifters and timing chain (whatever they were). And, even though it didn't look like much on the outside (it was a patchwork of green and blue with splashes of grey), he assured us that it would eat up the road as if it were candy.

'Okay, get in,' Danny yelled, as he turned the

engine over.

Alyce stood up and walked down to the passenger's door. She looked at me the roof as she yanked it open. A flicker of a smile touched her mouth and I nodded.

We're okay, I thought as I opened the door on my side. We slid into the car and giggled as we bumped up against each other. I hugged her quickly and said to Danny, 'Let's go, Brockie.'

Jack was waiting by the garage doors and when Danny gave him the thumbs-up, he pushed the doors open and we moved into the sunlight. When the car was all the way out, Jack closed the doors again and then jumped into the front seat.

Getting out of the yard was the trickiest bit of our little adventure. If Mum or Dad saw us rolling down the street in Mr Parish's car we were screwed, but I didn't happen. When they were playing bridge, the earth could have spun backwards and they wouldn't have noticed. Still, Danny took it slow until we cleared our street and were headed out of town.

It was a perfect afternoon for racing. The sun was hanging low, its fiery rim dipping behind the hills, leaving Prospect Road partly in shadow. A breeze from the ocean, laced with salt, blew through the scrub driving the stench from the dump back into the west. The only distractions were the birds with their endless screeching and squabbling as they fought over their last beak-full of garbage before darkness forced them to their nightly roosts.

We parked the Lancer under an old ghost gum opposite the dump - it would be the finish line for the race - and waited for Lilly to show up. Alyce and I lounged in the back, our feet sticking out the window, sharing a cigarette while we talked about our favourite movie stars and boys. Danny and Jack were fiddling around under the bonnet.

'Don't screw up anything under there,' I warned them, leaning out the window.

'We won't, Mira,' Danny called, from somewhere beneath us.

Jack looked over his shoulder and glared at me.

I stared back.

He gave in first and crept back under the bonnet (like the rat that he was) just as Lilly and Sebastian pulled in beside us. Sebastian jumped out of the car and stalked over to me. 'Whose bloody idea was this?' he demanded as I climbed out of the Lancer.

'Not mine,' I said, nodding towards Lilly. 'Have you asked her?'

Lilly climbed out of the Supra. 'Shut up, Sebastian. You heard Daddy, the car's half mine, so I can race it if I want,' she said.

I smiled to myself. She hadn't told him about our little bet.

'I don't care if it is half yours, you shouldn't do this, Lilly. It's dangerous. What are you trying to prove anyway? You know you'll beat him.'

Danny dropped the bonnet and wiped his greasy hands on a rag hanging out of his pocket, before sliding behind the wheel and starting the car. It grumbled into life, but soon smoothed out. He climbed out and ran his hand gently over the roof, as though he was patting his favourite dog. Then he nodded at the Supra and smiled. 'We could take that heap of junk any day.'

'See, the idiot wants to race,' Lilly said.

'Don't worry about my brother, Sebastian,'

Alyce said, brushing past Lilly. 'He's going to wipe the floor with your sister.'

Sebastian threw his hands up, exasperated. 'You're all frigging crazy,' he said, rounding on Lilly. 'If you do this and the car gets totalled, you're taking the heat from Mum and Dad.' He walked away and stood with his back to his sister.

Lilly clapped her hands. 'Fine. So, where do we start from?'

I left them to work out the rules - not that there would be many - and went over to Sebastian. 'We'll get a better view from over there,' I said, taking his hand. He pulled away but followed me across the road to where Jack already waited.

The cars roared off in a shower of dust and squealing tyres. They stopped at the agreed-upon point and turned around. Lilly was in the left-hand lane, Danny was in the right, and between them stood Alyce, her arms raised above her head.

'This is so fucked up,' Sebastian muttered, kicking gravel into the scrub behind us. He glared down the road and then fumbled for his mobile and flipped it open. But, before he could hit the call button, Jack grabbed the phone out of his hand.

'Don't ring her now. She needs to be thinking about what she's doing.' He looked past Sebastian, into my eyes, and said, 'She's got a race to win.'

At that moment, I noticed a smear of grease on Jack's hands and saw, just for a second, a glint of hate in his eyes.

'What have you been up to, little brother?' I asked.

Jack slowly rubbed at the grease as he glanced down the road to where Lilly and Danny were revving their engines. 'Nothing,' he said, as Alyce dropped her arms and the cars leapt forward, like cats after prey.

Danny had her for the first thirty metres and then, suddenly, everything went wrong. The Lancer jerked wildly and a cloud of steam billowed out from beneath its bonnet. The little car seemed to buck and then it came to a shuddering stop.

I couldn't believe it. I'd just lost everything in a belch of greasy steam. And Lilly - who hadn't noticed Danny or didn't care - just kept coming.

This was all Jack's fault.

The noise from Danny's car had disturbed the ibis feeding in the dump and, as Lilly bore down on us, a huge flock took off. The air above us was thick with the sounds of flapping wings as the birds lifted towards the sky in a mad panic.

'Look at that,' Sebastian said.

But I wasn't interested in the birds and neither was Jack. His eyes were glued to Lilly as she came flying towards us and, although I couldn't see his face clearly, I knew he was smiling.

Smiling! When that fucking cow had just shattered my dreams.

Now I'd be stuck in this hellhole forever, working in a goddamn *pharmacy* with my goddamn *father* for the rest of my stupid life. Never to be discovered. Never to be famous. Never to be a star like Kylie or Madonna or Nicole Kidman. I squeezed my eyes shut against the hot tears that boiled inside me. Girls who worked in pharmacies didn't become movie stars or pop princesses, they never got to perform in front of thousands of screaming fans, or win golden statuettes, or make guest appearances on late night TV. It just wasn't fair!

I don't know exactly what happened next - I was so mad that my mind sort of went blank - but I think I must've stumbled in the loose gravel. I reached out towards Jack, so I wouldn't fall, and the next thing I knew, the air was filled with the shriek of tyres, so loud that it overpowered the cries of the ibis. There was a sharp crack and a wet thud, followed by more squealing and a final, devastating crunch. Then there was silence.

I lifted my head slowly and saw Alyce and Danny running towards a lump in the middle of the road that was dressed in Jack's baggy denim shorts and faded blue shirt. Its legs were bent at odd angles. Beyond the lump, there was a car wrapped tightly around the ghost gum and beyond that was Lilly, sprawled between the tree's twisted roots.

Suddenly, sound crashed into the world again as though God had turned up the volume on his stereo: screams from Alyce and Danny as they reached Jack; groaning metal and the hiss of water leaking over the hot engine, and the cries of the ibis as they flew into the dusk.

'Mirrrraa!' Alyce screeched, her voice rising and rising, until I thought it would split my head open.

Christ, how I wished she would just shut-the-fuck-up.

Jack was trying to sit, but Danny held him on the ground. Alyce was yelling into her phone and waving frantically at me. I started walking towards them but, before I could get to Jack, Sebastian dragged me over to Lilly. He was sobbing and the front of his shirt was covered in blood.

For one heart stopping second, I thought he was

hurt.

But, as he dropped to his knees and pulled Lilly into his arms, I realised it was *her* blood. It had leaked out of her crushed body from a gaping wound in the top of her head.

'We have to fix it,' Sebastian pleaded, trying to force the two halves of her skull back together.

I closed my eyes and hid in the darkness, hoping it was all a dream, knowing it was not. I felt dizzy and I struggled to get myself under control. How could this have happened? I shook my head, trying to clear my thoughts, and then opened my eyes.

Sebastian had stopped trying to repair Lilly's shattered skull. He just sat in the blood-soaked dirt and rocked her, his eyes staring into nowhere. I stepped towards him and bumped into Alyce. She grabbed my shoulder and shook me.

'Damn it, Mira! What are you doing? Jack's legs are broken.' She shook me harder. 'Did you hear me? They're both broken!'

I pushed her off me. 'Lilly's all broken,' I said.

Alyce looked around me and I heard her suck in a mouthful of air. 'Ahhh, God,' she murmured.

'Will you stay with him?' I asked.

She nodded slowly, never taking her eyes from the twins.

Danny was sitting beside Jack, holding his hand and talking softly. He looked up as I approached. His face was pale and sweaty, his eyes as murky as the sea after a storm. I sat down on the road next to him and hugged him. I felt his chest hitch.

'Is… is he dead, Mira?' he asked.

I looked Jack over, blinking away the tears that wanted to blind me. The jagged tip of a bone poked through the skin of his left leg and his right foot was facing the wrong way, as though he was a puppet with tangled strings. A huge lump was rising, moon-like, on the side of his head and his lips had a bluish tinge. My eyes drifted down to his chest and I waited for him to breathe. Nothing.

Fear crawled along my skin as I shoved my fingers against his throat and felt around for a pulse. Nothing. Damn it, how did they do this on TV? I pressed deeper into his flesh and felt his pulse jump against my fingers. A harsh, barking laugh of relief burst from me.

'Mira?'

'It's okay, Danny,' I said, taking off my jacket and placing it gently over Jack. 'He isn't dead, just passed out. That's all.'

'Oh,' he replied. He brushed a curl away from Jack's face and went on with his mumbled prayer.

In the distance, I could hear the wail of the Bay's only ambulance. 'Help's on the way,' I said, squeezing Danny's hand.

As if he had heard me, Jack moaned and his eyes fluttered open. He stared into sky until he found a single, lonely ibis tracking its way to the west. He followed it, his head turning slowly, until his eyes locked onto mine.

'Hi, Jackie,' I said, softly.

His hand crept out from under my jacket and tugged on my T-shirt, pulling me towards him until our faces were almost touching. 'You pushed me,' he croaked.

'What? Are you crazy?' I protested, as his hand fell away from me and his eyes rolled back into his head.

I sat beside him until the ambulance came, holding his hand, waiting for him to come around again, so I could tell him the truth. But he didn't come round, not for another couple of months and, by that time, the truth no longer mattered.

THIRTEEN

Life went on in Harvest Bay after the accident. The sun rose and set, the tide rolled in and out, dolphins played in the channel beside the break-wall. The shops opened, cars drove through the streets, and empty fishing trawlers headed out to sea and came back full.

But, at the same time, everything had changed.

Everyone blamed me for what happened to Jack, even though I had nothing to do with the accident and it was Lilly who was driving the car. They never said anything out loud, but I could tell what they were thinking. I first noticed it a couple of weeks after the accident, at the prayer vigil that Mum's bible group had organised for Jack.

I plodded into the church behind my parents, who were immediately swamped with hugs and gentle words of encouragement, but when it came to me, people just whispered behind their hands and stared at me with their hard, angry eyes.

Only the Holborns seemed capable of understanding and sympathy. Even in the middle of their grief over losing Lilly, they opened their arms to me - something my own parents hadn't done - and hugged me as if I was their lost daughter. That raised a few eyebrows in the congregation.

Not that my mum or dad noticed. They were too busy talking into the mobile phone, no doubt checking to see if Jack had twitched in the last half an hour.

I know that sounds kind of harsh but I'd spent every damn day at the hospital with them since the accident, watching them as they watched over Jack, all the time feeling about as important as the shadows beneath his bed. I sat quietly in the corner while they held Jack's hand and talked to him about any mundane thing that came into their heads. Mum murmured stories about his life as she brushed aside the locks of greasy hair that fell over his pale face, telling him about the day he was born, his first day at school and the time he had chicken pox.

Dad mostly talked about running (surprise, surprise), keeping Jack up-to-date with who was performing and who had 'thrown in the towel'. Sometimes, he told him jokes and laughed, but his eyes never left the heavily bandaged legs, pinned within their sturdy metal brackets, that stuck out from beneath the crisp white sheet. And, every now and then, he would swipe away a tear as it rolled down his whiskered cheeks.

I tried to comfort them but they didn't really need me there. In fact, I don't think they even really wanted me in Jack's room, which made me wonder what they thought I was going to do to their precious boy. Smother him with a pillow? Block his I.V. line? Inject him with air? As if I could do something like that while they were in the room. Didn't they watch TV?

Their indifference to my presence and my pain upset me, but it wasn't surprising. I'd been coming second to Jack for as long as I could remember. What did surprise me was the way the rest of the town reacted when they saw me at the vigil: the whispering, the unforgiving looks, the shuffling to the end of the pew to prevent me from sitting in a particular place as if I was a black child riding on a whites only bus in a time of segregation.

Then there was my sixth-grade teacher, Mrs Bailey, with her sad look-what's-become-of-you eyes and our family doctor Peter Heddron (same look); the Hancocks (no peering down my top today) and even Mr Harris, my ally at the pharmacy, who turned his head away when I sent him a small smile during the ceremony. And let's not forget Alyce. She clung protectively to Danny - who threw me a kiss and proved that he, at least, still loved me - and refused to even glance my way.

Well, fuck the lot of you, I thought, as I slipped into the pew beside Sebastian. I hadn't seen him for a few days, not since his family had taken Lilly 'home' to Brisbane to be buried. He looked tired and of sort washed out, like a faded pair of jeans. I took his hand and squeezed it as Father Michael began his sermon. His lips twitched with a half-hearted smile. It was better than nothing.

The ceremony went on and on until just about everyone in town had offered up their prayers for Jack: *Please Lord, bring Jack home. Please God, make Jack whole again. Holy Mother, watch over our Jack.* Puke! Puke! Puke!

Some of their prayers were for my parents and quite a few were for Lilly and her family. I even got a mention or two - it wouldn't have been very Christian-like to leave me out completely, I guess - and then, after almost two hours, they were done.

As we filed out of the church (more hugs for my parents), I decided that I wouldn't be going to the hospital any more. Why should I waste my time when my parents acted like I didn't exist and everyone else treated me like a leper? The way I saw it, I could just as easily stay locked in my room and let them hate me. But, as the weeks slipped by, I realised there was no escape from the town at home either.

My parents continued to go to the hospital every day but in shifts - Mum one day, Dad the next - and whenever one of them was at home, their friends would stop by to keep them company. They'd sit around our kitchen, drinking tea and talking quietly about Jack, but whenever I came in, a wall of silence would come down and they'd look at me like I was some bug-eyed alien. Then they'd look at my parents as though they'd been cursed with the devil's own child. It's a wonder they didn't fork the evil eye at me.

When their silence became too much for me, I'd sneak over to Sebastian's house. His family had sort of taken me under their wing in the weeks following the accident - especially Clare, who sometimes called me Lilly in a way that freaked me out, but I let it go 'cause I knew she was grieving and all that. The Holborns didn't blame me. *They* knew shit happened sometimes and they welcomed me into their home, which became a kind of sanctuary where I could escape the town's anger.

At least, until a 'For Sale' sign was rammed into their front lawn.

My heart leapt as I walked up their driveway, past the red and yellow sign, and squeezed between the boxes that were stacked up beside the open front door.

'Hello?' I called.

The usually spotless house was a mess and, in the middle of the chaos, was Sebastian's mum. She looked up and I could see she'd been crying.

'Come in, Mira,' she said, waving me towards Sebastian's room.

'Are you okay, Mrs Holborn?' I asked.

She held a framed photograph of Lilly in her hand. 'No, but I will be soon.' She picked up the wine glass sitting beside her, climbed unsteadily to her feet and weaved towards the kitchen.

Sebastian had told me that she'd started drinking again but I hadn't seen any sign of it until now. Her ash-blonde hair, usually held in a tight knot, fell in clumps from a loose bun set ridiculously high on her head. She was still in her silk pyjamas, the pretty cherry coloured ones that I liked, but she had thrown an ugly mint-green dressing gown over the top making her look like an oversized boiled lolly. Her feet were bare. A smear of something -it looked like chocolate - made a fat comma on her chin and a packet of potato chips lay open on top of a cardboard box, as though she had gotten an attack of the munchies while packing.

I looked down the hallway to Sebastian's room and sighed softly. Then I followed Clare into the kitchen, just catching her by the elbow as she kicked the corner of the doorway and stumbled.

'Damn it,' she yelled, hobbling over to the bar stools that were pushed under the breakfast bench. As I helped her to sit, the vinegary smell of wine rising from the pores of her skin filled my nose.

'Are you all right?' I asked her, as she leaned against me and lifted her foot.

Clare giggled as she wriggled her toes. `Nothing broken here,' she said, and then a sob ripped from her. 'Only something broken in here.' She thumped her hand against her chest as her tears came faster.

I held her close to me, not really knowing what else to do, and after a while, the tears began to slow again. When she had stopped completely, Clare drew away from me without speaking and took a tissue from a box on the bench, blowing her nose in the delicate and refined way of the rich.

Her reflection grew in the stainless steel door of the fridge as she crossed the kitchen and yanked open the door. She lifted a bottle of wine from the shelf and topped up the glass that she had been carrying around like a deformed appendage. She took a large swallow and then topped up the glass again before returning the bottle to its place in the door. When she looked at me again, her face was calmer and more controlled, but grief still gathered in her eyes like a storm on the horizon.

'I apologise for my behaviour, Mira. It is a difficult time for me. For all of us,' Clare said, coming over to me. 'But it's not like I'm telling you anything new; what with your brother in hospital and your parents caught up in their worry and grief, too busy to protect you from the viciousness of this intolerable town.' She put her glass on the bench and gripped my arms, 'I would never have allowed them to treat our Lilly so callously.'

'I'm just lucky that you're here,' I said in a quiet voice, my eyes blurring.

Clare wrapped her arms around me and hugged

me tightly, stroking my hair as she murmured, 'Lilly. Oh, my Lilly.'

We stayed that way until William gave a quiet cough from the doorway. He didn't seem surprised to find his wife hugging me and I realised that he must have been watching us for a while. Clare wiped one hand quickly over her face while the other crept along the bench and clenched the wine-filled glass.

I stepped away from Clare, unsure of what was about to happen.

'Hello, Mira,' William said, giving me a smile that was both warm and sad as he walked over to his wife and gently took the glass from her.

Relief rushed through me. 'Hi, Mr Holborn. We were just—'

William shook his head. 'There's no need to explain,' he said, patting my shoulder before he turned to Clare. 'I think it might be time for a rest, my darling.' He spoke in a soft, coaxing voice as he slipped his arm around her shoulders and guided her towards the door.

~

For a moment Clare looked longingly at the glass left on the bench. 'Yes, I guess so. Thank you for coming by, Mira. I'm sorry if I upset you.'

'You don't have to apologise for anything, Mrs Holborn.'

At the doorway, she stopped and looked back at me. 'Sebastian's a bit down today, Mira. Will you see if you can cheer him up?'

'I'll try,' I replied.

'Thank you.'

As William took Clare through the house to their room, I picked up the wine glass and, for a second or two, I was tempted to down its contents in one quick gulp. Instead, I tipped the wine down the sink, rinsed the glass and set in on the sideboard to dry. I turned and gave a silent prayer of thanks when I saw William leaning against the door, watching me.

'Another good decision,' he said, as he ambled over to the pantry and brought out a bag of coffee. 'Would you join me one in of these?' He opened the packet and breathed deeply, as the aroma of macadamia nuts and chocolate floated through the kitchen. I smiled a little, remembering a time when the only thing the house smelt of was geriatrics' piss. How things had changed.

'Thank you, Mr Holborn, but I don't drink coffee.'

'No problemo,' he replied and barked out a laugh. 'Isn't that what you young ones say today?'

'Sometimes,' I said, with a shrug as I edged towards the kitchen door. 'I think I'll go and see Sebastian now, if that's okay.'

'Of course, but could I just say—' his hand squeezed the coffee bag convulsively, 'the time you have spent with Mrs Holborn in the last few weeks, since our girl... since this whole terrible thing—' He rubbed at the frown that creased his forehead into a synoptic chart and took a deep breath. 'What I'm trying to say is that I think you have been good for my wife. Your visits have helped ease her pain and get through this mess. And, just... well, thank you.' He turned away abruptly and began to spoon coffee into the cappuccino machine.

I stood where I was for a moment, wondering how to respond. Yeah right, I guess that's why you're moving out of town I wanted to say, but I kept the thought to myself. Instead, I walked over and kissed him lightly on the cheek, just like I used to do to my dad, before I scooted out of the kitchen and down the hall-way to Sebastian's room.

His door was ajar and I pushed it open. He was lying on his bed, headphones clamped over his ears, his eyes closed. I walked over and touched his arm softly, trying not to scare him.

He jumped anyway. 'Shit!' he said as he yanked the headphones off his head.

I smiled and plonked down beside him. I didn't feel like playing games so I got straight to the point. `So you're moving, huh?'

Sebastian nodded. 'I don't want to, but Mum says she can't stand living in the Bay any more. She wants to go back to Brisbane.' He pulled me down into his arms and I cuddled into his side.

'What about us? I asked, trailing my fingers across his stomach.

'I don't know,' he muttered. He turned his head towards the window and a deep sigh lifted his chest. 'I told them I wanted to stay, you know, because you're here. But Dad said if it was a choice between what I want and what Mum wants, he has to make her happy.' He laughed bitterly as he looked back at me. 'Suddenly he gives a shit about how she feels, and it only took Lilly dying to make it happen. How fucking hilarious is that?'

I propped myself up on my elbow and gazed into his face. There was no hint of humour in his dark eyes, only pain and anger. The muscles of his jaw were bunched beneath his skin and I rubbed them gently. 'I could go with you,' I suggested.

Sebastian looked at me. 'Would you do that?'

'In a heartbeat.'

His face broke into a grin - the first I'd seen in weeks - but it faded almost as quickly as it had appeared. He sat up and swung his legs over the side of the bed. 'What about your mum and dad?' he asked.

'They'd be happy to get rid of me,' I assured him, sitting up and moving to sit next to him. 'Besides, they've got Jack to keep them busy. What about your parents?'

'Don't worry, it won't take much to convince them. They love you almost as much as I do.' He put his arm around me and held me tightly. 'I couldn't stand losing Lilly and you,' he whispered and then he kissed me.

A few days later, our families got together for the last time.

It was so different from Christmas. There was barely a smile between us, no laughter rising through the branches of the jacaranda, and our conversation was as forced as that of strangers sharing a compartment on a train. Eventually we gave up on the polite chatter and got down to talking about Brisbane.

It was a short discussion. Mum and Dad listened carefully as Clare delivered a passionate (and somewhat embarrassing) speech about the benefits such a move would have for everyone. Then, my parents excused themselves and went into the kitchen to make coffee. When they came out again, five minutes later, my future had been decided. I was going to Brisbane with the Holborns.

'But this will always be your home,' Mum told me, reaching across the table to take my hand.

'That's right, the door's always open, Mira,' Dad agreed, taking my other hand.

A rush of love and doubt swept through me as I looked into their tired haunted faces. *Maybe I should stay*, I thought, *maybe they really do need me?*

Then, the phone rang.

I don't think I've ever seen my parents move so fast. Their hands were snatched out of mine as they shoved their chairs away and charged back into the kitchen. I felt like yelling, 'Don't run in the house!' just as they used to yell at Jack and me when we were kids, but the words couldn't get passed my clamped lips.

Clare and William reached for me at the same time, each taking one of my hands, which had been left like fish floundering on the sand by my own parents. They smiled at me - warm, understanding smiles that instantly made me feel better - and I realised that my life would soon be back on track.

Although they never told me straight out, I could sense that my mum and dad were secretly relieved that I was going away. There was, despite the tears that flowed down Mum's face as I climbed into the Holborn's car, a tension between us and I knew they still blamed me for Jack's injuries.

But, that was their problem.

I knew the truth. Jack had messed around with the Lancer so that Danny would lose the race and I'd have to stay in the Bay. He didn't want me to be free to chase my dreams while he was still running in circles, trying to make our parents happy. It was Jack who was responsible for the accident, and my parents' shattered dreams, not me.

I was just a girl trying to make her own dreams come true.

Email #4

Retrieved from laptop belonging to: William Holborn (Age 52)

Point of Origin and Authorship Indeterminable

From: <lizzy@borden.com>

To: <fallingstar@email.com.au>

Sent: Saturday, 3 October 2013 3:45PM

Subject: Fw: On Fame and Fortune

My Dearest Mira,

An interfering family is ill suited to the pursuit of fame and fortune. Dance a bloody dance, sing the murderous song, let the blade swing long. Fear not the consequence, for immortality will be your reward.

Miss L. Borden.

Assessment: The Borden email was recovered from a laptop belonging to William and Clare Holborn. It was received some time during the final days of Mira Falling's residence in their home. An investigation into the origins of the email proved inconclusive. However, it is possible that it was sent from Harvest Bay. Authorship of the email, like the others received by Mira, remains a mystery.

FOURTEEN

I'd been living in Brisbane with the Holborns for almost nine months when Sebastian's mum sprung her offer of an all-expenses-paid holiday on us. It was a strange thing for her to suggest and I was immediately suspicious because I knew that, in the time I had spent with her family, Clare Holborn had come to hate me.

We were lazing around one morning, sipping coffee and eating freshly baked croissants, when Clare stepped onto the patio where breakfast was always served. She carried a plate of toast and a silver dish of curled butter, which she placed on the table as she slipped into the chair opposite us.

'Don't you two look cosy this morning?' she remarked, delicately buttering her toast. Sebastian smiled, but I watched her guardedly, wondering why she was being nice.

'It's not like you to join us for breakfast, Mum. Is there something wrong? Sebastian asked.

'No, not at all. On the contrary, I have a surprise for you,' she said, pausing dramatically. 'A week's holiday in Sydney.' She sounded like a game show announcer revealing the major prize; all that was missing was the wild applause.

Sebastian's eyes lit up. 'That'd be great,' he said, leaning over to hug Clare. She accepted his embrace with a delighted smile that turned my stomach. Then Sebastian took my hand, 'What do you think, Mira? Feel like hitting the club scene in Sydney?'

I looked at Clare who was innocently nibbling on her toast. 'I guess so,' I said.

'And, while we are down there, maybe we could check out that drama school you're always on about.'

Despite my suspicions, my heart sped up a little. 'Do you mean NIDA? Could we really? You know, it's the best drama school in the country.'

'Yeah, I know. You've only told me a hundred times,' he replied, with a smile.

'Maybe you could take in a museum or an art gallery while you're down there,' Clare put in.

'Yeah, right, Mum,' Sebastian smirked.

'Oh, I see. If it doesn't appear on a screen, then it's not worth seeing. Is that it? Heaven forbid that you should do something cultural for a change, Sebastian.' She picked up her plate of toast and excused herself.

'Mum?' Sebastian said.

'Don't worry about her,' I said, turning his face towards mine. 'So, why do you think your mum's offering us a week away?'

'I don't know. Maybe she's in a good mood,' he said, kissing me quickly, but not quickly enough to prevent his mum from catching us.

'That's enough of that,' Clare snapped from the door. Deep lines of disapproval creased her forehead and I knew there was something more to her offer than just a simple holiday. Especially after the argument we'd had only a couple of days earlier when she'd caught me in her husband's study.

I'd gone into the study to use the laptop so that I could email Alyce. I hadn't heard from her since I'd left Harvest Bay; she wouldn't answer my texts or take my calls, and I was desperate to know how she was going. I turned the laptop on and email program but before I could think of what to write, an email popped up on the screen. I thought it was for William (it *was* his laptop) but then I saw my name.

Was William talking about me behind my back? And just who was he talking about me to?

I crept over to the door and opened it a crack to make sure no one was coming. The hallway was empty and the house was quiet. I closed the door and went back to the laptop. As I scrolled through the email, I realised that it wasn't about me. It was for me, and it really freaked me out.

It was from Lizzie Borden. I knew who she was and what she'd done. I even remembered the rhyme we used to sing about her in primary school as we jumped over Alyce's skipping rope:

Lizzie Borden took an axe,
And gave her mother forty whacks.
When she saw what she had done,
She gave her father forty-one.

What sick bastard would send me an email pretending to be Lizzie Borden? I thought of Jack straight away, but I hadn't spoken to him in ages. Why would he start up his old tricks now? And how did he know I would be on the computer at this exact moment?

My mind spun as I remembered the other strange emails I'd gotten over the years: one from N.K., one from Saucy Jack, one from Bonnie Parker and now one from Lizzie Borden. Was I missing something? Maybe Jack hadn't sent them, but who else could it be?

I frowned at the screen. Did I have a serial cyber-stalker with a mass-murderer complex? It was possible. Hell, people all over the world impersonated dead rock stars and dead movie stars. And what about the chicks who had plastic surgery so that they could look like Barbie - seriously weird - or fans who took other drastic measures so that they could masquerade as their favourite celebrity?

Ned Kelly, Jack the Ripper, Bonnie Parker and Lizzie Borden were some of the most famous people in the world - they had what my mother called 'iconic longevity' - and their stories had been told over and over again on film, in music, art, books and theatre. Would it be so strange then for some lonely geek-boy to send me emails while pretending to be these people?

'Yes, it would,' I said, and shivered. Especially as it now seemed that he had some sort of telepathy that allowed him to track me down, no matter where I was or what computer I was on.

I shook my head. No, there had to be a simpler explanation. *Maybe the mails really had come directly from the 'other side'* I thought, and giggled a little. Now that was just straight out creepy.

I read the email through again - what family was it referring to? What the hell did it mean? - and then I tried to delete it, but it came back, as if it was trying to remind me of something important.

It was all too weird, even for me, and I reached for the power switch on the laptop. That was when Clare walked into the room and busted me.

She ordered me out of the study, as though I was a dog that had pissed on her favourite rug. I lowered my head, hiding the anger that coiled like a snake inside me. I pushed the chair into the desk and sneaked a look at the laptop screen. The message was gone and I breathed a sigh of relief.

At least, the whining bitch couldn't use that against me. I tried to slip past her into the hallway, but she wasn't finished with me.

'You know, Mira, maybe it's time that you thought about going home. I spoke to your parents the other day and I think they could really use your help in the pharmacy.'

I looked at her steadily. 'Are you saying I'm not welcome here anymore, Clare?'

'Of course not. It's just that good jobs are very hard to find. And, let's face it, nothing has come of your... um... career objectives.' She tilted her head and laughed— just like Lilly.

'Well, maybe if I had a bit of frigging support.'

'I believe you've been very well supported for the last year, Mira,' Clare said. Her voice was polite, but the creases around her eyes deepened with anger. 'We have done all that we can for you and I think it's time you considered your other options.'

'And what about Sebastian?'

She folded her arms across her chest. 'I'm sure he will survive without you. He is a Holborn, after all.'

I tried to tell Sebastian that his mum was out to get me but, since she was always nice when he was around, he wouldn't believe me. And he didn't see anything sinister about her encouraging us to go to Sydney together, either. I knew she was up to something, however, and I was pretty sure it had to do with getting rid of me.

FIFTEEN

We left Brisbane early in the morning after crashing with Sebastian's oldest friend, Ryan Hart, for the night. Clare had wanted us to stay at the house but Sebastian convinced her that it would be easier to get out of the city from Ryan's apartment, which was in the Valley and not far from the highway, rather than fighting through the traffic from Bethnal Green, the outer northern suburb where his parents lived.

His mum had reluctantly agreed, leaving us free to party with our friends for a few hours, before we headed back to Ryan's place for a couple of drinks and a - relatively - early night.

Not that I got much sleep. I always find it hard to relax in unfamiliar places and I spent an hour or so tossing and turning before I finally got up and went for a walk down to the Seven Eleven. I bought a Slush Puppy and chatted with the middle-aged attendant while I spooned the icy treat into my mouth (his name was Chester and I'm sure he had a hard-on by the time I left the store), then I wandered back to the apartment.

Sebastian had crashed out on the lounge and I stood over him for a minute, listening to the sound of his breathing, before creeping back to the bedroom where sleep eventually found me.

As a result of my restless night, I was still tired when we set out the next morning but nothing could have dampened my excitement as we cruised through the peaceful inner suburbs, slipping past houses where people were still sleeping or just waking to face the day. Sleepy, unsuspecting people, oblivious to our existence as we prowled among them.

Have you ever thought about how vulnerable you are when you're sleeping? In that all-consuming blackness, where you don't see or hear or smell or feel? When a killer could be standing over you, watching you breathe and deciding if you should live or die?

I used to think about that a lot. I'd stay awake all night trying to catch the murderer as he slipped into my room. But no one real ever came. Sometimes, as I sat staring at my reflection in the mirror at the end of my bed, I would imagine that Saucy Jack or Bonnie Parker had come for me. I would hear the click of a gun, or see the glint of a knife slashing through the air, and I'd dive under my blankets, cursing my brother for sending me those goddamn awful emails.

By the time we cruised out of the city, most of Brisbane was awake and shuffling into another pointless day. We dodged semi-trailers that materialised around us, belching fumes as they roared down the freeway. We cursed half-awake businessmen in their Volvos and laughed at mothers who, with perfect make-up - even at that time of the day - chauffeured their protesting kids to another day of forced schooling. We pulled free of them, finally, and flew down the liquorice strap highway that rolled out before us, music thumping. We sang and joked and held hands as we raced along the coast, stopping only when we needed to stock up on essential supplies, and petrol. Then we'd take off again.

By late afternoon, we were halfway down the New South Wales coast and getting close to the turn-off to Harvest Bay.

The car suddenly filled with tension and our upbeat mood soured. I could feel Sebastian accelerating a little more with each passing road sign, until the turn-offs were flashing by in a blur. The Old Coast Road, which led into the Bay, was gone in a blink as we screamed through the T-section.

I reached over and squeezed Sebastian's arm and he jumped under my touch. 'Take it easy,' I said, and some of the grimness slipped from his face and the car began to slow.

'Sorry. I didn't think it would be so hard being this close to where Lilly died.'

'I know. I feel it too,' I said, as I shifted in my seat and pulled at my cargo pants.

Sebastian glanced down at my legs. 'Let's take a break.'

'Good idea, I can feel the blood pooling in my butt,' I said, making him laugh as I wriggled around to get my circulation going.

'We swung into a truck stop a few kilometres past the Harvest Bay turn-off and picked a parking space in front of the cottage-style restaurant. The smell of grilling burgers and hot chips wafted out through the screen door and made my stomach gurgle as I climbed out of the car.

'Guess that means you're hungry?' Sebastian said, sliding out from behind the steering wheel. He stretched his arms above his head and groaned with pleasure as his back made little popping noises. I walked around the back of the car and wrapped my arms around him, slipping my hands under his shirt and gently raked my nails across the firm flesh of his stomach. I felt him shiver.

Although I didn't trust his mother's motives, I was happy to be spending some time with Sebastian on my own. It gave us the opportunity to really get to know each other -something we couldn't do at his house, which was about as private as a railway station. Especially when Clare was around.

I'd never meet anyone who partied as much as that woman. Brunches and lunches, intimate dinners, political fund-raisers with hundreds of guests. She just never stopped.

It wouldn't have been so bad except whenever she 'entertained' she'd treated me like her personal slave. It was always, `Mira, do this. Mira, do that' and I'd be running from the minute I got out of bed. Folding napkins, dusting shelves, washing windows, driving to the super-market for smoked salmon and Camembert cheese - just like bloody Cinderella.

I guess that was the price I had to pay for hooking up with her precious son. Or maybe that was the way rich people like the Holborns thought a small town girl like me should be treated. But, then again, there was that thing with Lilly - not that any of that was my fault.

We sat in a booth near the window, not talking much, lost in our own thoughts, until the food came. This was the closest I'd been to home in nearly a year and it felt strange to be driving past without stopping to see my family. Not that they'd be pleased to see me.

The burger was good - thick and juicy - with heaps of chips on the side. We wolfed them down, and then slowly fed each other chips and bits of salad until the red-headed woman behind the counter looked like she was gonna puke.

Jealous bitch.

When we'd finished, Sebastian paid the bill and we wandered outside. 'I'm going to get some water,' he said.

'Okay, but don't be too long. I might die of loneliness,' I replied.

Sebastian laughed and walked over to the shop.

He was so cute. And I don't just mean the way he looked (although he was pretty yummy). He had style and ambition. He wasn't like the boys I grew up with; boys with no plan for their lives other than following their fathers into the fishing business. Some girls might find that attractive, but not me. I had bigger plans and Sebastian was going to help me achieve them.

I watched him through the shop window as he pulled the water out of the fridge and swaggered over to the register to pay for it. A woman in a loud yellow and purple dress was talking to the shop assistant, so he put the bottles down and waited for her to finish. Suddenly, his body tensed and he stood perfectly still, staring at something on the counter.

I groped for the door handle, wondering what he'd seen to make him act so strangely. Was it a gun? A knife? Was he standing in the middle of an armed hold-up?

Then, he reached forward and picked something up. I craned my neck, trying to get a better look, and I saw that it was a newspaper. My heart began to pound and I chewed on my bottom lip as Sebastian turned jerkily, like a puppet in the hands of an amateur, and walked out of the shop.

He stopped in the shadows of the awning and stared at me - as though he'd never seen me before - and I sat back in the soft leather seat, waiting; knowing that whatever was in that newspaper wasn't going to be good, least of all for me.

Internet Archive Search:

The Northern Guardian

Late edition, 26 November 2013

BRISBANE COUPLE FOUND MURDERED IN BED

Residents of a north Brisbane suburb were in shock yesterday after the savagely beaten bodies of a social-ite couple were discovered in the second-floor bed-room of their home.

Police said robbery appeared to be the motive behind the attack on the 52-year-old man and his 46-year-old wife.

The whereabouts of the couple's 19-year-old son and his 18-year-old girlfriend are unknown and police have expressed concern for their safety.

'We have launched a search for the teenagers and hope to contact them shortly,' said Detective John Neil of Bayer Hills CIB.

The victim's names have not been released.

SIXTEEN

Sebastian stumbled out from under the awning, the crushed newspaper in his hand. His shoulders were stooped as if he carried some terrible weight and he stared blankly at me as he approached the car.

I popped my door open and climbed out. 'What's wrong?' I asked, as he came around the bonnet and shoved the newspaper into my hand.

'I think it's my mum and dad,' he said. His knees buckled and he slid to the ground beside the front wheel.

I spread the paper out on top of the car and read the headline and the brief story below. I couldn't believe it. This could ruin everything, I thought, screwing the paper into a tight ball.

I knelt down beside Sebastian and wrapped my arms awkwardly around his shoulders. His body was stiff, as though he'd been transformed into a statue, and he stared across the parking lot.

'What are you thinking? It's not them,' I said, trying to comfort him. 'Your parents aren't the only people who live in the northern suburbs, you know.'

His head turned slowly towards me. 'Did you read the story? Who else could it be?'

Voices drifted across the driveway and I took a quick peek through the window to see what was going on. The shop assistant, the woman in the loud dress and a couple of other strangers, were coming towards the car. The redheaded waitress stepped through the restaurant's door and lit up a cigarette as she crossed the bitumen to join them.

'Is everything all right, Miss?' she called, through a swirling cloud of smoke when she spied me.

I ducked down and grabbed Sebastian by the arm. 'Come on, we've got to get out of here,' I said, dragging him to his feet and helping him into the car. I scrambled past the small crowd of people and slid behind the wheel, slamming the door shut on their stupid, prying questions.

I kicked the engine over and let it idle, ignoring the frowning faces outside the car, while I tried to figure out where to go. I wanted to take Sebastian somewhere quiet, so we could work through this thing with his parents. The only place I could think of was home.

I hesitated a minute longer. I didn't really want to go back to the Bay. Not like this. I was supposed to be rich and famous before I walked those streets again, but there was nowhere else to go. I burned out of the truck stop, showering the onlookers with gravel, and headed back up the highway to the Old Ocean Road.

Sebastian paid no attention to where we were going at first, but then he noticed the McIntyre River winding along beside us and he suddenly sat up. 'Turn the car around, Mira,' he demanded. 'I'm not going to Harvest Bay.'

'But—'

'We're going back to Brisbane. I have to see my parents,' Sebastian said, pulling on my arm.

The car swerved onto the soft shoulder and I fought the wheel, dragging it back onto the road. 'Hey! Don't do that,' I snapped, shrugging him off.

'My parents are dead!' he yelled. 'Now, turn the fucking car around.'

'You don't know that,' I replied, trying to stay calm.

'Mira…' Sebastian said, his voice tight.

I looked over. His eyes were grim, his mouth compressed, his hands clenched.

'Okay,' I said, softly. 'But you can't drive all that way in your condition. You'll kill us. Let's just go somewhere for an hour. Get our heads together and, when you're a bit calmer, we'll go back.'

From the corner of my eye, I saw his hands relax slightly. 'I don't want to stop in the Bay,' he said.

'I thought we could go to my parents.'

He grunted. 'Yeah, I'm sure they'd have the welcome mat out for us.'

'Time heals all wounds, Sebastian.'

'Not the ones that put you in a wheelchair.'

'Shut up,' I said. He could be such a prick when he was angry. 'If you don't want to go to my parents, then where can we go?'

'I just want to go home,' he said as we rounded the last bend before Harvest Bay.

Nothing seemed to have changed in the time that I had been away. McGinty's caravan park, as overgrown with weeds as ever, still had more rusting cars and tractors than visitors. The bridge over the McIntyre still rumbled in protest as we drove over it. Potholes still ate away at the narrow road.

'Go to the lighthouse,' Sebastian blurted out.

'The lighthouse? I don't think we should go up there.'

He gave me a black look. 'No goddamn arguments.'

'Fine,' I grumbled.

It was a good idea, really. The lighthouse would be deserted, so we could be alone. That would give us a chance to get this situation with his parents into perspective and, once we had that cleared up, I knew I'd be able to convince him that we should keep going on to Sydney. And from there, who knew where we might go?

SEVENTEEN

Sometimes, the best way to be anonymous is to hide where everyone can see you. So when Sebastian and I drove into Harvest Bay, we headed straight down Main Street, past my father's pharmacy and the pizzeria, past the street where we had lived - where my parents and brother still lived - and out along Prospect Road, as if it were the most natural thing in the world.

The locals were used to outsiders cruising their streets, but I was still glad the car had tinted windows. No prying eyes. No wagging tongues. No chance of spoiling my *real* homecoming when I was rich and famous.

I thought Sebastian might lose it when we passed the gum tree on Prospect Road where Lilly had died. But he just sat, hunched against the door, staring moodily out of his window.

Until a flock of ibis swooped over the car.

He pressed his face against the window and watched them as they wheeled and dived towards the dump. I heard him sniff and I wondered if it had been a mistake to make him come here.

But, damn it; he didn't belong in Brisbane, just like I didn't belong in the Bay. With his money and my talent, we could do something special with our lives. All he had to do was take a chance and cut his family lose. I was his family, now. The only family he'd ever need.

As I'd expected, the lighthouse was deserted. I parked the car on the seaward side, facing down the cliff, where no one from town would be able to see it. We sat quietly, staring out across the ocean, watching the white-capped waves roll onto the coast. The long green and brown grass whispered beside the car, rustling in the sea breeze that rushed over the cliff, while a solitary seagull rode the slipstream, screaming.

'So, we're here. What now?' Sebastian asked, keeping his eyes fixed on the soaring bird.

He looked like a sulky kid, scrunched down in his seat, arms folded across his chest, refusing to look at me. He was so cute, I wanted to laugh but that would have made him angrier, so I swallowed my laughter and shuffled around in my seat until I was facing him. 'Now, we talk,' I said.

'There isn't anything to talk about,' he replied, smashing his fist onto the dashboard, making me jump. 'I should never have let you talk me into coming here. It was a stupid idea.'

'No, it was a good idea. In the first place, you're totally stuffed and if you tried to drive back to Brisbane now, you'd never make it. And what good would that do? Another Holborn to stick in the ground - at least you'd be reunited with Lilly, I suppose.'

Sebastian flinched, as though I'd sliced him with a razor, and glared at me.

'Look, I'm sorry. I just don't want anything to happen to you,' I said, putting my hand over his arm.

'Please, Sebastian, what will it hurt to talk for a while?'

He just stared out of the window. 'There's nothing to talk about. I want to go back.'

'To what? Your dead parents?' I demanded, snatching my hand away.

His head whipped around. 'So you do think they're dead!'

'What if they are?' I yelled. 'Why should you fucking care? You've spent a whole year telling me that you can't wait for them to drop dead, and now that something might've happened to them, you want to run home. If they're dead, Sebastian, then they're DEAD, and there's nothing you can do about it!'

I didn't mean for it to come out that way. I know it was harsh, but it annoyed me that he'd suddenly developed a conscience. Why were people always trying to spoil my plans for the future?

Sebastian stared at me, his dark eyes smouldering. He opened his mouth and snapped it shut again, as though he didn't trust what would come out. I reached over and tried to take his hand, but he shoved me away and opened his door.

'Just fuck off, Mira,' he said, as he climbed out of the car. He slammed the door, making the car shudder, and walked down the hill to the security fence.

Crap. Crap. Crap. This was not going how I had planned it.

I opened the driver's door and got out. The wind swept through my hair, reminding me of another day I had spent up here. And suddenly I realised that there was a way to make Sebastian take me to Sydney.

I walked down to the fence and stood beside him.

He was leaning against the railing, his head resting on his arms. I touched him on the shoulder but he ignored me.

'I'm sorry,' I said, climbing over the railing. 'I'm an idiot. I should think before I say stuff that I don't mean. Please don't be angry with me, Sebastian.'

He straightened up and looked past me to the ocean. 'Some of what you said is true. I have wished my parents dead plenty of times and, maybe, that's part of why I have to go back, but that's not the only reason. If it is them in the news story, then the police will be looking for me, and there will be…' he hesitated and wiped his mouth with the back of a shaking hand, 'arrangements to make. I can't just forget about that and go off with you. Even if I wanted to.'

I took a step away from the railing. 'But you haven't heard about the surprise I've organised for you.'

He frowned at me. 'Are you listening to me at all? I'm going home,' he said, looking down at the railing separating us. 'What the hell are you doing over there?'

'Playing a game,' I said, shuffling backwards.

'Are you nuts? Get back over here and quit being stupid.'

'Come and get me,' I replied.

'No way. And if you don't get your arse back over here, I'm going to drive off and leave you.'

'You leave and I'll jump.' I took another step away from him.

The wind howled over the cliff, tugging at my shirt and cargo pants. It pushed and dragged at me, and I stumbled over the rocks. It was a lot stronger than the last time I'd been up here with Jack, Alyce and Danny.

Maria Arena

'Mira!' Sebastian shouted.

'It's okay,' I laughed. 'I've done this plenty of times.' I sat down on the edge of the cliff, my legs dangling into emptiness and patted the cold, uneven rock next me. Sebastian looked uncertain but relieved that I wasn't walking around anymore. 'Come on. Just hear what the surprise is and then, if you still want to go back to Brisbane, we'll leave. Straight away, no more excuses. Okay?'

'All right,' he said, scowling as he climbed over. 'If it'll get you in the goddamn car.' A blast of wind ripped away his next words as he sat down beside me. He looked kind of nervous.

'What was that?' I asked.

He leaned towards me. 'This is the stupidest thing you've ever asked me to do, Mira.'

'Oh, come on! Where's your sense of adventure? It's beautiful up here, like sitting on top of the world.'

He glanced around. 'Yeah, it's just great. So, what's the surprise?'

I sighed. He wasn't much of a romantic, but I loved him anyway. I reached into the back pocket of my cargoes and brought out a silver key. It was hanging from a star-shaped key ring that flashed in the sun. I shuffled closer to him, so he could hear me over the crashing waves and roaring wind.

'I've rented us an apartment in Melbourne,' I said.

'What?' he asked, his eyes wide and confused.

Excitement bubbled in my belly and I couldn't hold back any longer. I grabbed his hands and held them tightly. 'I wanted to tell you sooner, but it was supposed to be a surprise. I was surfing the Net a couple of weeks ago and I found this real-estate site that was renting an apartment in Fitzroy - very ritzy - and it's just perfect for us. I thought we could spend a couple of days in Sydney and then drive down to Melbourne.'

'That's your surprise? A *holiday* unit?'

'No, not a holiday unit, silly.' I slapped him playfully on the arm. 'Our own place.' I stared out over the headland, imagining our lives together. 'We'll get jobs and I can take acting classes maybe at the Victorian College of the Arts. It will be hard at first, but we can make it, I know we can.' I turned towards him and the excitement I felt withered as I saw the suspicious look on his face.

'How did you manage to rent a unit in Melbourne?'

'It was easy,' I explained, laughing a little. 'The only tricky part was getting the references - I had to tell a little white lie - but when the agent realised that his new tenants were Holborns... well, he was happy to accept the bond.' I wrapped my arm around his waist and squeezed. 'So, it's all arranged. When we get to Melbourne, we'll be living together! How cool is that?'

'Where did you get the money for the bond?' Sebastian asked.

'What does it matter?' I said, annoyed. He wasn't listening to me. I was trying to explain how great our life was going to be and all he could think about was money.

He took my arm from his waist and shifted around until he was looking into my face. 'Where did the money come from, Mira?' he asked again, in a voice as sharp as the wind howling over the headland. Suddenly, his eyes narrowed as the answer occurred to him. 'You've been stealing from my parents.'

'No! I earned every damn cent of that money.'

'When did you earn it?' he demanded. 'You haven't worked a day since you moved in with us.'

'Have you been listening to me?' I snapped. 'We're going to be living together. No more interfering parents, just you and me, doing what we want with our lives.'

'The money, Mira,' Sebastian yelled. 'Where did you get it?'

'Okay, okay. If that's all you care about. I got it from your mum.'

'Bullshit. She'd never give you money.'

'She didn't give it to me. It was payment for all the goddamn work she made me do around the house. All those hours of cleaning and picking up after her and your dad.'

'She paid you?' he asked, unconvinced.

'Not exactly.' I took a deep breath, trying to stay calm. 'I took what she owed me and I used the money to buy us a future. If that pisses you off, then, I guess it's just bad luck.'

'That's so low,' Sebastian said, staring at me coldly. 'How could you steal from my parents? Don't you have any fucking morals?' He stood up and started walking back towards the fence.

I jumped to my feet, sending a shower of small stones over the edge and, for the second time in my life, I found myself wavering on the brink of death. I wheeled about, trying to keep my balance. Then, like an actor moving in slow motion, Sebastian swung around and leapt towards me. He stretched his arm out, his fingers catching the front of my shirt, and pulled. I heard something tear and then I skidding across was the rocks.

The only sound in the world was the blood pumping through my head. Then Sebastian was standing over me. 'You stupid bitch! You scared the shit out of me,' he shouted. I looked up at him and his face softened when he saw the tears welling in my eyes. He sucked in a deep breath and held his hand out. 'Are you okay?' he asked, as he yanked me to my feet.

'What were you going to do? Keep your threat to drive away and leave me here?' I asked.

'No. I was just going to cool off, that's all,' he said, kicking a loose rock over the ledge.

'I'm sorry about the money. I guess I didn't see it as ripping your mum off. And I thought you'd be excited about moving to Melbourne with me,' I said, letting the tears fall.

'Ah, Mira,' he said, pulling me into his arms. 'I probably would've been, and maybe the money wouldn't have mattered, if my parents weren't—' I felt him swallow, hard. 'But even if things weren't so fucked up, what about my job and my friends? Did you think I could just leave all that behind?'

'You would if you loved me,' I said, against his chest.

'You know I do, but it's not that easy. I… *we* have responsibilities.' He sighed. 'Now more than ever.'

I knew then that he was going back to Brisbane and that he expected me to go with him. But I couldn't. Not with his parents there - What if they were dead? I've never had the stomach for funerals; all that sadness and grief is just so *morbid* - and not when I had my own place waiting in Melbourne.

After all, a girl has to follow her dreams.

I pulled out of his arms and stepped away. I looked up at him standing on the edge of the cliff, wrapped in the golden glow of the sun, his hair whipping around his face and I wondered whether I was making the right choice. Maybe my dreams could wait a while longer. But I'd waited so long already and every day that slipped past felt like an eternity between me and the life I wanted so badly. I had to make a choice.

'So, you won't go to Melbourne?'

Sebastian shook his head.

'Well, in that case, you can go to hell.'

EIGHTEEN

Sabastian was gone. After all we'd been through, he dumped me like a puppy in a sack and left me to fend for myself. I sat against the safety fence for a long time, staring across the water, trying to accept that he'd bailed out on me. Like an idiot, I'd thought that he loved me more than anything or anyone. But, in the end, he'd chosen his parents, as if they were more important than me.

The rim of the sun had just slipped into the sea when I finally got myself moving. As I trudged up the slope, a cold wind blasted across my back, raising goose bumps along my arms. I hugged myself and wished desperately for Sebastian. But, then, some part of me wailed, 'Screw him!' and I pushed him out of my mind.

I was almost at the top of the knoll when the beacon in the lighthouse suddenly flashed on, sending a beam of warm yellow-white light spearing into the gloom.

The lighthouse was transformed.

It had always been an ugly building, short and squat, like a giant toad (not at all like the sky skimming towers in fairy tales). Its white paint was cracked and peeling where the salty air had lifted its plastic skin, and its roof, once as red as a clown's nose, was faded to the colour of dried blood. But, at that moment, as I stood on the bluff with my teeth chattering, it looked like the most beautiful building in the world.

I hurried over to the door at the bottom of the tower. It was padlocked, but that had never stopped me before. I found a good-sized rock and, after a few hard whacks, the rusty lock burst and I went in.

The lighthouse had two levels. The first floor was a large round room, empty except for shadows and an old grease-caked engine squatting against one wall, which oozed oil onto the dusty concrete. Partially hidden by the engine was a metal staircase that spiralled up to the second floor.

I climbed the stairs, holding tightly to the railing that was bolted into the wall. At the top, there was a landing that circled the beacon. I walked around, looking through the thick panes of salt-encrusted glass.

From one side of the tower, I could see the lights of Harvest Bay twinkling in the distance. Most of Beachmere, though, was hidden by the rise of the headland and I could only see a couple of isolated houses and, strangely, the tips of the masts of the fishing fleet.

On the ocean side, there was a line of thick, black clouds (which explained why the trawlers were sheltering in over each other and the harbour) that seemed to roll grow larger as they raced across the sea.

Great, I thought, as I stared out at the approaching storm. *That means I'm stuck here for the night.* Damn Sebastian! If only he hadn't pissed off on me.

We could've been in Sydney, getting ready to go out and have some fun. God, what a jerk.

I sighed and turned my mind to making myself comfortable for the night. At least I'd be dry, though, as the rumble in my stomach reminded me I was beginning to get hungry again and my throat felt as though it was coated in dust. My exploration of the tower hadn't turned up anything to drink or to eat - except for the fat brown cockroaches that scuttled around the base of the beacon and I wasn't going to eat them, no matter how nutritious they're supposed to be.

I looked through the windows just as the beam scraped the top of the keeper's cottage. I swallowed and felt a dry click at the back of my throat. *There probably won't be anything to eat in there either*, I thought, *but there should be some water*.

The keeper's cottage was linked to the lighthouse by an overgrown white-pebbled path that glowed eerily in the light from the beacon. My dad told me once that the pebbles were whales' teeth, collected from the bottom of the ocean by the ghosts of sailors, who placed them on the path so that the lighthouse keeper could always find his way between the two buildings, especially on stormy nights. It was a stupid story, but I was glad the path was there, as it was quickly getting too dark to see.

No one had lived in the cottage for a long time and it had been turned into a sort of museum for whatever nautical crap washed up onto the beaches along the coast. My mum used to organise tours for anyone interested enough to make the trek up to the headland and, in the summer, there'd always be some dick from the city banging on our door, demanding that Mum open up the lighthouse and cottage so they could have the Harvest Bay 'cultural experience'.

Whenever that knock came, Jack and I would bolt out the back door and disappear for the afternoon. Mum would be seriously pissed off by the time we got home, and we'd be grounded for a couple of days, but anything was better than playing tour guide to a bunch of urban morons.

As with the lighthouse, a large padlock protected the cottage but it was rusted and flimsy. *Good on you, Mum*, I thought, *how do you expect to keep anyone out of here with this?* I jogged back along the path until found the rock I had used earlier on the lighthouse door and, within a couple of heartbeats, I was inside.

The cottage was haunted-house dark, so I wedged the door open to let in the light from the beacon, which swept over the cottage about every ten seconds. It was glint of metal during one of these sweeps that I saw a from behind a cabinet on the far side of the room.

I walked through the cottage, pushing aside the piles of junk that lay around the room: rusty bells, brass nameplates, snapped masts and a rudder or two. My mum called that stuff 'artefacts of the sea'. I called it crap that should have been left at the bottom of the ocean to rot.

The gleam I had seen from the door came from a metal buckle on the strap of a backpack. It had slipped behind the cabinet and, for some reason, had become wedged about halfway down. I pulled on the strap and tried to wriggle the bag free but no matter what I did, it refused to budge.

By now, my mouth felt like sandpaper and I was

having trouble working up enough spit to lubricate my throat. I had to find something to drink. I glared at the cabinet in the gloom and turned to the small kitchen that was to the left of the front door. Its cupboards were bare but there was a tap over the grimy sink that worked and I slurped at the rust-flavoured water and washed my face.

With my belly full, I felt a little calmer and I decided that I should spend the night in the lighthouse (at least I wouldn't be completely in the dark).

As I headed for the door, the sparkle of the buckle caught my eye again and I knew I wouldn't be able to settle for the night until I had the bag in my possession. I leaned against the side of the cabinet and tried to shove it out of the way but it was as swollen and heavy as a bloated carcass, and when I gripped the sides, the wood crumbled away in my hands.

Frustration ate at me as I pushed the rubbish off the top, not caring about its 'historical significance', then I yanked out any drawers that weren't warped shut and dropped them on the floor. I danced about, grimacing with disgust as small things skittered across my feet, but I wasn't going to give up. I wanted that bag and whatever was in it.

I grabbed the cabinet by its back corner, digging my fingers into the wood as though it was flesh, and pulled. It slid noisily across the floor for an inch or two and then stopped. That was okay, though, because I heard the bag drop to the floor with a thud.

I smiled in the dark as I lifted my prize onto a table and yanked open the drawstring. I plunged my arm inside and groped around, my searching fingers finding what felt like a pen and maybe a notebook, and a small square object that I couldn't identify. I withdrew my hand from the bag and tossed it over my shoulder, thinking that it might contain something that could help pass the time until morning. Maybe I'd use the pen and paper to write a letter to my family. Or maybe I'd write a confession.

Or not.

Outside, the storm had swallowed the day and the first fat drops of rain were splattering against the windows. I bolted out of the cottage, leaving the front door open, and followed the path back the lighthouse.

Sitting on the cold platform upstairs, safe from the rain that battered the headland, I examined my discovery. The bag was old and faded, with bare patches on the bottom where the canvas had worn thin. A pocket on the front, rimmed with a rusted zipper, was half open and empty. One of the straps was broken, just below the metal buckle, while the other was held together with a small army of staples.

I tipped the bag upside down and a pile of junk clattered onto the landing: a notebook, pens and a couple of stubby pencils, a creased map of NSW, a disposable camera, a postcard and — a small round packet, wrapped in pink and silver paper.

My stomach gurgled as I picked up the Lifesavers. There were only three left and the top one was covered with little bits of lint, but I didn't care. I ripped off the wrapper and shoved them greedily into my mouth, sighing as the sweet taste of musk spread across my tongue. I closed my eyes and slowly sucked on the lollies until they had dissolved completely. Only then did I look at the other things in the bag.

The camera was pretty useless. There was only one shot left on the roll of film, so I took a close-up of a wad of chewing gum I found stuck under the railing and shoved it back into the bag.

The notebook was more interesting. It was full of sketches: pencil drawings of lighthouses and associated buildings, set on jagged rocks or against ocean back-grounds that stretched to a charcoal horizon. Flicking through the pages, I recognised the lighthouse and the keeper's cottage on Disaster Point, but there were many others that I'd never seen before. On the back of each page was a name - Warden Head, The Iron Pot, Crookshaven Point - and a date. I looked at the drawing of my lighthouse and saw that it had been done two days earlier.

'I wonder if someone's realised that the bag is missing yet?' I mused, as I sat back against the beacon, the metal casing warm and comforting, and turned to the last few blank pages in the notebook.

There were many hours to kill before morning so I thought I might try my hand at sketching the lighthouse too. At least it would stop me thinking about my current predicament. I soon gave up though, when I realised that drawing is not one of my many talents.

I put the notebook aside and picked up the postcard. On the front was a snapshot of a street lined with shining gold stars. I sighed as I recognised the Hollywood Walk of Fame. *Will I ever have a star of my own*? I wondered as I flipped the postcard over. On the back was written:

The brightest shine the eternal night;
The questing suffer the day.
Fame, the jewel within their grasp,
Only to slip away?

'Great,' I said and flicked the card away, suddenly feeling alone and as though my dreams were as distant as the sun. I drew the notebook towards me, thinking that I would write a letter to Sebastian. Although he was probably halfway down the coast by now, maybe by putting my thoughts on paper, I would feel a little closer to him.

I dragged the bag over to where I was sitting and fluffed it up into a pillow. I lay down on my stomach, staying close to the beacon, and thought for a long time about what I would write.

Finally, I began. Dear Sebastian…

The pencil quivered against the paper, leaving a short, ragged mark like a knife wound. My eyes grew heavy and I blinked, trying to stay awake but it was useless. *I'll just rest for a minute*, I thought, snuggling into the bag, and when my eyes opened again, I was staring into the grey light of a new day.

NINETEEN

A car was winding its way up the hill towards the lighthouse.

It might have been silver, like Sebastian's. It was hard to tell. I shifted nervously from one side of the tower to the other, trying to get a better look but, in the early morning light, everything looked as washed out as a pair of old man's undies. I couldn't even tell what make or model it was, but it seemed big and official looking.

It was travelling fast too, as if it couldn't wait to get to me. Was it the cops? Or the owner of the notebook? Or just another stupid tourist from the city, racing to catch the sunrise?

I gnawed on my bottom lip. Either way, it wasn't Sebastian.

Behind me, the beacon suddenly winked out and the grinding noise that had comforted me all night slowly dwindled into silence. Now, there was only the sound of the ocean pounding against the headland and the drone of the vehicle.

Then, without warning, an ibis crashed into the glass in front of me, as if God had thrown it out of the sky. I screamed and jumped away from the window.

The bird seemed to shake itself in mid-air and then it flew off towards the Bay.

I pressed my head against the cool glass and waited for the jack hammering in my chest to subside. A myriad of thoughts raced through my head, like a tape running at high speed: Jack in the running blocks, his face a mask of concentration; Alyce coughing up a lung the first time we tried cigarettes; Danny with a streak of grease on his cheek; Lilly, her pretty mouth twisted into a cruel smile; and Sebastian coming out of the sea.

But where was he now?

I looked out of the window and searched the sky until I found the ibis that had crashed into the lighthouse. It had turned away from Harvest Bay and was heading towards the dark and distant range. As it disappeared into the shadows, I was filled with a realisation.

'It's free to go wherever it wants,' I murmured.

I knew, then, that I couldn't stay any longer. Sebastian wasn't coming back and I'd have to go on without him. After all, I still had my dreams to achieve and nothing could be allowed to stand in my way. Not friends, or family or boyfriends. And certainly not an arsehole in a silver car - unless he wanted to give me a lift to Sydney.

Then it would be a whole different story.

EPILOGUE

The only noise in the room came from the other side of the doorway.

Shouts, giggles and loud conversations; mumbles, sobs and wails of despair; footsteps skittering madly down the hallway, followed by the squeak of rubber-soled shoes in pursuit. Mira's room, however, was silent.

She stood at her window, arms folded across her chest, looking out over the garden with its lush lawns and flowering shrubs. To one side was a tennis court, with no nets, and a swimming pool surrounded by a barbed wire topped fence.

A circle of women sat on the grass, talking. Mira knew what they were saying - the therapy sessions were always the same. She should've been out there too, but she'd been given the morning off for the visiting hour.

The door behind her opened and the sounds of the ward swelled and rolled into the room.

Mira turned slowly. She didn't speak or look at her visitor. Instead, she allowed her eyes to fall on the manuscript that had been tossed on her bed. The small gold stars embossed on its cover glittered in the sunlight that spilled through the bars on her window.

Her visitor watched her. 'You don't like it?' he asked finally.

Mira chewed at her ragged thumbnail. 'Things didn't happen that way,' she said. 'And you know it.'

Jack rubbed a hand over his eyes and gave an irritated sigh. 'I wrote it the way you told it to me.'

Mira gazed at him. She remembered sitting in the garden with Jack, talking about their childhood - that was part of her therapy - but she was sure she wasn't responsible for the events that had occurred in Harvest Bay all those years ago.

Jack rolled his wheelchair to the bed and reached for the manuscript, but Mira beat him to it. 'I'll take that,' she said, retreating to her desk.

Jack shrugged and sat back. He studied his sister as she flipped through the pages, shaking her head when she came to a part she disagreed with.

Mira didn't know how lucky she was to be in Pleasantview. It had cost Jack a small fortune to get her into the prestigious institution; not that he begrudged her the expense. Mira needed help. He looked down at his useless legs, a smile on his face. After all, he knew exactly what she was capable of.

Mira turned the manuscript towards him. 'Where did you get these?' she asked, pointing to an email.

'Dr Llewellyn gave them to me. I think he got them from the police. They searched our house, you know. Mum was terribly upset by the whole thing.'

Mira flipped to the back of the manuscript. 'What about this one from Lizzie Borden? That wasn't at our house.' She looked at him through narrowed eyes.

Jack held up a hand. 'I don't know where the police collected their evidence from. I only used what was in your file.'

'Sure you did,' Mira said, lifting a stack of papers from her desk. 'Or maybe you had the original emails that you sent to me when we were kids? Just like you've got the originals of *these* stashed somewhere!' She threw the papers onto the bed.

Jack leaned across and picked up the scattered sheets. Famous names leapt out at him - Kurt Cobain, Michael Hutchence, Marilyn Munroe, Virginia Woolf - and he frowned.

'What are you trying to tell me, Jack?'

'You think I sent these? God, we've been through this a million times, Mira. I haven't sent you anything. I didn't even know you had a computer in here.'

Mira ignored Jack's protest and began to pace about the room. 'You *want* me to commit suicide, just like they did,' - she flicked her hand at the emails - 'because if I did myself in, that would help the story, wouldn't it? That's why you sent them. You want me dead, don't you?'

Jack threw the emails back on the bed. 'No, I don't want you dead, Mira, although some people might think I've got good reason to,' he said, unconsciously rubbing his legs. 'And I didn't send those emails.'

'Then who did? A bunch of dead people?'

'Maybe you sent them to yourself?'

'Why would I email myself?' Mira sneered.

'I don't know, but I think it's something you should talk to Dr Llewellyn about.'

Mira turned back to the window. The women on the lawn had gathered their chairs and were making their way towards the main building, some racing ahead or running in looping circles, some dragging their feet at the back of the group. It made Mira sad to look at them. She took a deep breath. 'I suppose you're going to put these new emails in the story.'

'No. I like it the way it is,' Jack replied.

'But it's all lies,' Mira snapped. 'You've changed everything to protect your precious reputation as a writer.'

Jack rolled his chair closer to the door. 'It was my reputation that got the manuscript accepted by a studio.'

Mira whirled around, her long hair flying out like a cape. 'What studio?' she demanded.

'That's not your concern. All you need to know is that I'm going to make you a star.'

Mira scrambled over to him and knelt beside his wheelchair. 'Not with this,' she pleaded. 'I can't be the star of a lie!'

'What does it matter, Mira? You're going to be famous, or should I say infamous.' Jack sniggered. 'And isn't that what you've always wanted? Your name in lights. Your place among the stars.'

'Yes, it is. But... I'm not responsible for the things in here,' Mira shouted, flinging the manuscript away from her as though it was a disease-covered rag.

Jack looked at her with an expression that was almost gentle. 'Stop lying to yourself, Mira,' he said, as he banged on the door, which was opened by a sour-faced orderly. He rolled into the hallway and turned back to Mira. 'You can keep the manuscript,' he offered, as the door slowly closed. 'Think of it as a souvenir.'

Jack pressed a button on his wheelchair and an electric motor hummed into life. The hint of a smile touched his lips as he weaved down the corridor, his mind occupied with thoughts of how he might, at last, turn his fallen sister into a Star.

Acknowledgements

The author gratefully acknowledges Associated
R & R Films for permission to reproduce an extract
from *Gallipoli*.

SISTERHOOD

MARIA ARENA

Abandoned by her jet-setting mother at St Mary's Boarding School for Girls, Heather Johnson thought life couldn't get much worse. She was wrong. Waiting for her behind the iron gates is an ancient evil, embodied in the insidious Sister Merce and her coven of malevolent Sisters, who thrive on the misery they inflict upon their wayward charges.

As the danger to Heather increases, a reprieve arrives with Amy, a spirited girl with a strange flair for Latin. The respite, however, is fleeting as Amy's physic abilities reveal a mystery involving two long-dead 'fallen' girls, Jennifer and Rachel. Using a diary and an amulet, and assisted by the sweet-hearted Patrick and self-destructive Caleb, the four girls are drawn into a liminal space where they must stand together and use the power within themselves to destroy the Sisterhood.

Suspenseful and enigmatic, *Sisterhood* pits the darkest aspects of human nature against its greatest virtues.

To purchase *Sisterhood* as an e-book, visit: Amazon Google Play or Smashwords

To read more about Maria Arena, visit:
www.mariaarena.com.au